Kristen asked, peering at Grant curiously.

He cleared his throat. "I'm fine."

But he wasn't fine. He knew he wasn't fine. He was nuts. Stark raving mad.

His gaze securely fastened to hers, Grant wondered what would happen if he kissed her. There was a possibility he'd discover these urges were just his imagination.

But there was also the possibility that she'd taste as sweet as her personality.

"Okay. Then I'm going to my room," Kristen said.

"Great."

If he believed he was losing it, now he had to concede he'd already lost it because he had every intention of kissing Kristen. He didn't know how, he didn't know when and he wasn't sure why, but soon nature was going to take over, and he was going to cover her mouth with his....

BREWSTER
BABY BOOM

Dear Reader,

March roars in in grand style at Silhouette Romance, as we continue to celebrate twenty years of publishing the best in contemporary category romance fiction. And the new millennium boasts several new miniseries and promotions... such as ROYALLY WED, a three-book spinoff of the cross-line series that concluded last month in Special Edition Arlene James launches the new limited series with A Royal Masquerade, featuring a romance between would-be enemies, in which appearances are definitely deceiving....

Susan Meier's adorable BREWSTER BABY BOOM series concludes this month with Oh, Babies! The last Brewster bachelor had best beware—but the warning may be too late! Karen Rose Smith graces the lineup with the story of a very pregnant single mom who finds Just the Man She Needed in her lonesome cowboy boarder whose plans had never included staying. The delightful Terry Essig will touch your heart and tickle your funny bone with The Baby Magnet, in which a hunky single dad discovers his toddler is more of an attraction than him—till he meets a woman who proves his ultimate distraction.

A confirmed bachelor finds himself the solution to the command: Callie, Get Your Groom as Julianna Morris unveils her new miniseries BRIDAL FEVER! And could love be What the Cowboy Prescribes... in Mary Starleigh's charming debut Romance novel?

Next month features a Joan Hohl/Kasey Michaels duet, and in coming months look for Diana Palmer, and much more. It's an exciting year for Silhouette Books, and we invite you to join the celebration!

Happy Reading!

Mary-Theresa Hussey

Mary-Theresa Hussey
Senior Editor

Please address questions and book requests to:
Silhouette Reader Service
U.S.: 3010 Walden Ave., P.O. Box 1325, Buffalo, NY 14269
Canadian: P.O. Box 609, Fort Erie, Ont. L2A 5X3

OH, BABIES!

Susan Meier

Published by Silhouette Books
America's Publisher of Contemporary Romance

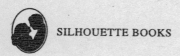 SILHOUETTE BOOKS

ISBN 0-373-19433-1

OH, BABIES!

SUSAN MEIER

has written category romances for Silhouette Romance and Silhouette Desire. A full-time writer, Susan has also been an employee of a major defense contractor, a columnist for a small newspaper and a division manager of a charitable organization. But her greatest joy in her life has always been her children, who constantly surprise and amaze her. Married for over twenty years to her wonderful, understanding and gorgeous husband, Michael, Susan cherishes her roles as a mother, wife, sister and friend, believing them to be life's real treasures. She not only cherishes those roles as gifts, but also tries to convey the beauty and importance of loving relationships in her books.

Grant,

You're a very demanding person, and though that's served you well all your life and probably made you more successful than your mother and I ever envisioned, you need to be careful with women's hearts. For Kristen's heart has been broken once.

A man as successful as you are, as good with people as you are, should be able to find a place for Kristen in your world. If she's anything like my Angela, she's bright, articulate, loving and kind. Surely you could use someone like her somewhere in your life.

Because I trust you, because I know you'll be compassionate enough to put petty feuds aside, I'm putting my kids in your hands... and hope you do the right thing.

I'm sure you'll know what to do.

Love,
Dad

Chapter One

"I think I must be lost," Kristen Morris Devereaux said to the butler who had answered the front door of the Tudor mansion. If her directions were correct, this was the home of Grant, Evan and Chas Brewster, the men from whom she wanted to get custody of her sister's triplets. She understood that the Brewsters were far from poor, but she hadn't expected them to have a butler and a mansion. If this was their home, they were people so far out of her social sphere she'd look like nothing but a country bumpkin to them.

For the first time since she discovered she wasn't alone in the world, she felt a stab of reality poke her enthusiastic bubble of hope. Still, she held her smile in place. She had to do this.

"I'm looking for the Brewster residence."

"This is the Brewster residence," the butler responded.

"Good," she said, though inside her spirits sank. She forced herself to smile again. "I'm Kristen Devereaux."

For a few seconds, the man only stared at her, obviously taking in her appearance from head to toe and pausing on her simple red dress which wasn't shabby or disgraceful, but probably didn't meet the standards of people who could afford a butler.

His questionable inspection strengthened her will. After suffering the loss of her husband, then her only sister, Kristen had learned life wasn't always easy. With so much at stake, she had resolved to be tough, persistent, even downright pushy if she needed to be. If he was trying to shatter that confidence, he'd have to do much better than peer at her as if her clothes confused him.

He did.

He smiled.

One small upward movement of his lips shifted the angles and planes of his face, transforming him from a gatekeeper bully into Prince Charming at the ball. The brown eyes that were so suspicious became warm and welcoming. With his beautiful shiny black hair, black beard and absolutely perfect face, he was the epitome of tall, dark and handsome. Over six feet, but not bulky or too well muscled, he wore his tuxedo with an easy grace, a languid sexuality. Her gaze ambling up his beautiful body and returning to his face, Kristen suddenly recognized he was gorgeous, and all her self-assurance fluttered away like the four-and-twenty black birds exiting the pie.

"Hello, Ms. Devereaux," he said kindly, extending his hand to shake hers, setting off an odd chain reaction of tingles that started in Kristen's stomach and spiraled downward to her toes.

When he released her hand, he smiled at her again. "Can I take you out to speak with Lily?"

"Lily?" Kristen asked, breathless and baffled. She didn't have a clue who Lily was, but more than that, from this gentleman's sexy smile she could tell he was a charmer—probably somebody well accustomed to having women fall at his feet. Though that should have automatically repelled her, Kristen felt another unexpected jolt of pleasure because the look on his face also told her he found her as attractive as she found him.

"Lily, the bride." he said, grinning foolishly.

Kristen squelched the urge to close her eyes and groan out loud. *The bride?* Oh, for Pete's sake! This guy wasn't the butler. He was a member of a *wedding party*. She'd arrived just in time for a wedding! He thought she was an inappropriately dressed guest and from the way she was ogling him he also thought she was so smitten with him that she'd forgotten the bride's name.

Great. Just great. Even before she explained who she was she'd made a fool of herself.

A smart woman would take herself and her inappropriate red dress into town to find a room for the night and return in the morning when all the festivities had died down. Sounded like a darned good idea to her.

"Actually I'm—"

"Here you are, Grant."

Wearing a tuxedo and looking every bit as relaxed and regal as the gentleman at the front door, the man who interrupted Kristen appeared to be another member of the wedding party. As if only noticing Kristen, he gave her a polite, apologetic smile. "I'm sorry to interrupt. I'm Evan Brewster," he said, extending his hand to shake hers.

Suddenly realizing she was in the thick of things, Kristen's heart thumped and her limbs turned to rubber, but she took Evan's hand and returned his smile. "Kristen Devereaux," she said.

"And I'm Grant Brewster," Grant said, nudging his brother aside. "My brother Evan is married. I am not," he said shamelessly. "Would you like to dance?"

"You don't have time to dance, Grant," Evan said. Even

as he spoke a short blond woman, probably in her sixties, shuffled up behind him, carrying a baby.

The child wore a frilly pink dress, white tights and shiny black patent-leather Mary Janes. Before Kristen could notice any real detail like the color of the child's eyes and whether she had the perfect pert nose of all Morris children, a tall red-haired woman appeared carrying another baby. This one was a boy. And behind that woman was a young, beautiful brunette, carrying another girl. This baby wore a dress identical to the dress the first baby wore, but this little girl's hair was pitch-black. And she had brown eyes as dark and as clear as Grant Brewster's.

Filled with wonder, Kristen only stared at the children while Evan Brewster spoke.

"There's too much excitement outside for the kids, and all three of them could use a nap. But Mrs. Romani can't handle them alone."

"I can't handle one baby alone," the seasoned blonde in the black leather miniskirt reminded gruffly. "I'm not even trying with three."

Grant sighed, but Kristen recognized his dilemma immediately. Both he and his brother were wearing tuxedos and the young woman holding the dark-haired little girl wore an autumn-orange gown. Obviously all three of them were in the wedding party.

And the babies were Kristen's sister's triplets.

Not only were they around the right age, ten months, but Kristen could see the green of Angela's eyes in the first little girl, and the boy had Angela's sandy-brown hair. These were Angela's babies. She could feel it in her bones.

"I could help with the children." Kristen heard herself say the words before she actually registered the thought. Because she was the triplets' aunt, and because the Brewsters were obviously preoccupied, it just seemed to make sense for her to be the one to take the children off their hands.

"If you're putting them down for a nap, all Mrs. Romani and I have to do is keep them company in the nursery until they fall asleep."

Grant's gaze traveled over to her slowly. He either couldn't believe that she had offered, or he wasn't sure he trusted her with the children.

From the long scrutiny she received from Grant and everyone else, Kristen was fairly certain it was the latter.

When he finally spoke, it was quietly. "Are you sure you don't mind? You haven't even had a chance to speak with Lily yet."

"I can speak with Lily later," Kristen said, not admitting she didn't really know Lily. Now that she was in the room with the family who controlled the fate of her nieces and nephew, and up against the knowledge that they were rich strangers who didn't have to trust her, certain truths about the situation became crystal clear. Once she told them who she was and that ultimately she wanted custody of these babies, they might not be as agreeable to letting her spend private time with the triplets as they were right now.

"They do need a nap," Mrs. Romani reminded tersely and, as if on cue, the little boy began to cry. One of the girls rubbed her eyes.

"And we should be outside with Lily and Chas," the woman in the orange gown said. "They can't handle all the guests on their own."

"I'm still working with the caterer," Evan interjected. "At this rate it will be another ten minutes before we eat."

"Okay. Okay," Grant said with a sigh, turning to Kristen again. "If you're sure you don't mind, we'd appreciate your help with the babies."

Kristen smiled. "It will be my pleasure."

The brunette handed the dark-haired little girl to Kristen and it was everything Kristen could do to keep from gasping with pleasure. Carrying the little boy, Grant Brewster accompanied Kristen and Mrs. Romani upstairs into the nursery, which was clean and bright, and decorated with rainbows and angels.

She wanted to hold the baby forever. Grant instructed her to lay the child in her crib. Reluctant, but resigned because she didn't want to draw any undue attention, she placed the little girl in her bed, slipped off her ruffly pink outfit and tights and dressed her in lightweight pajamas.

"What's her name?" she asked quietly as the baby rolled onto her side, wrapped the rim of a blanket in her small fist and began to drift off to sleep.

"Taylor," Grant whispered. "The little boy is Cody. The other girl is Antoinette. We call her Annie."

"Annie," Kristen said, smiling.

"If you two are okay, I need to get back downstairs," Grant said, turning toward the door.

"Yeah, yeah, whatever," Mrs. Romani said, shooing him out with her hand. "We're gonna be just fine."

He cast the woman a narrow-eyed glance, one that clearly told Kristen he wasn't overly thrilled with Mrs. Romani's gruffness, then left the room.

Mrs. Romani sighed with relief. "He's a tough one."

Kristen couldn't help it, she giggled. "Seems like."

"Oh, he's nice enough, but when it comes to these kids, he's a real pain in the butt. When I took this job I had every intention of working as both housekeeper and nanny—I could handle three kids in my sleep because I worked in day care—but that one, that Grant, he's such a nitpicker I didn't want the aggravation."

"He can't be that bad," Kristen said, taking a cue from Mrs. Romani and settling in one of the three rocking chairs far enough away from the cribs that their whispered conversation wouldn't disturb the kids.

"He's worse," Mrs. Romani said, pointing a stubby finger at Kristen. "That's kind of why I'm glad we got a minute alone...*Kristen Devereaux,*" she added slyly, looking directly at Kristen. "I haven't been with the Brewsters long, but when I clean I have access to absolutely everything. While I was storing some things in the basement cabinets for Chas a few weeks ago, I came across your name on papers in boxes of Angela Morris Brewster's things." She paused, holding Kristen's gaze. "I know who you are..."

Grant couldn't shake the feeling that he knew Kristen Devereaux. When he'd first seen her on the threshold of his home, he couldn't remember her name from the guest list, but he had to admit that once he got a really good look at her he wouldn't have cared if she *had* crashed the wedding. She was so darned attractive that he was absolutely speechless for a good thirty seconds. He hadn't met a woman who had had this kind of effect on him in years. Hell, he didn't think he'd *ever* met a woman who made his mind go blank the way Kristen Devereaux had.

"You seem to be well," Evan said, sidling up to his brother and handing him a tall, cold glass of beer, "not really angry, but not really pleased about something."

"I'm fine," Grant mumbled, accepting the glass from his brother. Though most of the guests were happily sipping champagne after dinner, Grant was a simple man who liked a good beer. The fact that his youngest brother remembered that was a sign of respect of sorts. The fact that his second brother brought him a drink when there were other chores to be performed was a sign that everybody noticed his mood.

Not good.

"You're not fine," Evan stated. "Because if you were, you would be enjoying the wedding. I always know when something's bothering you, because you stand around as if you're in a daze or thinking. Maybe thinking too hard when you should be celebrating?"

Grant couldn't help it, he smiled. "Something like that."

"So what's the problem?"

Oh, there was a good question, Grant thought, walking to a chair under an umbrella-covered table. How did one explain to his little brother, who was happily, joyfully, blissfully married, that he was annoyed because the woman who was currently watching the babies nap had set off alarm bells when she told him her name, but he ignored them because she was so darned good-looking? His first instincts put him on red alert, but he'd forgotten that warning sign when feathery blond hair, big green eyes and a slight Southern drawl brought other reactions to the forefront. Packaged in a trim red dress that accented a figure that would bring most grown men to their knees, Kristen Devereaux could have asked him for the family silver and he probably would have handed it over. *That* was what actually bothered him.

When Grant didn't say anything, Evan sighed. "Grant, for the first time in a long time, things are falling into place for us. The lumber mill is operating at peak performance. We found a housekeeper. Chas just married a wonderful woman. What could you possibly be worried about?"

What indeed?

Since Evan seemed willing to listen, Grant decided to give this discussion a shot. If he skipped the fact that he had ignored his internal alarm because he was incredibly attracted to Kristen and jumped to the more general aspects of the problem, like the fact that she was really quick to volunteer to sit with Mrs. Romani, maybe he did have a chance of getting his point across without looking like an idiot.

"Aren't you even the slightest bit curious about why Kristen Devereaux offered to baby-sit the kids?"

Evan's forehead furrowed. "Why should I be?"

"For starters, she hasn't even said hello to the bride yet."

"If she's a friend of Lily's and she realized Lily's wedding party was having a problem," Evan disagreed casually, "I think it's nice that she volunteered to help out. But she wasn't exactly dressed for a wedding. Did she say she was here for the wedding?"

"Why else would she be here?"

Evan took his time about answering, waving to a few distant relatives who sat at one of the round umbrella tables on the far edge of the patio. To keep everyone off the potentially damp grounds, tall pyramids of yellow, amber and auburn mums were strategically placed to encircle the stone floor. Potted red maples hid the in-ground pool. By the grace of God they had a warm sunny November day.

Grant glanced at the people who'd caught Evan's eye and he, too, waved. But even as he greeted people whose names he barely recalled, he realized his brother was stalling.

"Evan," Grant said, his brother's name coming out like a warning growl.

"All right," Evan said, exasperated. "Claire and I put an ad in all the Pittsburgh newspapers, advertising for a nanny. We'd had such good luck with the ad that brought us Mrs. Romani that I thought…"

"What do you mean we had such good luck with Mrs. Romani?" Grant gasped. "The woman *hates* kids."

"The woman *hates* you," Evan corrected, extending his arm over his wife's shoulders when she came over and sat on the chair beside his. "Isn't that right, Claire?"

Stunning in her burnt-orange gown, dark-haired, blue-eyed Claire looked him right in the eye. "I'm sorry, Grant, but sometimes you come across as being a little gruff."

"Gruff!" he all but barked.

"I rest my case," Evan said, then laughed.

"I give up on you two," Grant said, walking away because there really were a hundred more important details to attend to than sitting around discussing their cantankerous housekeeper and his disposition. For him there was no question that Mrs. Romani was a grouchy old bat. And he also didn't have to debate whether *his* disposition had gone to hell in a handbasket because he knew damned well that it had. He was a thirty-six-year-old man who'd just married off his youngest brother. He'd never, ever considered marriage for himself, but he had to admit—if only to himself—that during the ceremony he'd felt old and alone.

And right now, standing outside the French doors that would take him inside the house, and eventually upstairs to the nursery to give Kristen a reprieve from watching the kids, he couldn't help but wonder. Did seeing the spark of attraction in the eyes of a woman as beautiful and sexy as Kristen Devereaux cause him to ignore the nagging feeling that something about her wasn't quite right?

"I'm surprised it took you this long to get here."

Kristen peered at the curious housekeeper, wondering if she was making an enemy or an ally. Since she couldn't tell and expected everybody to know who she was in another two hours or so, she decided to rehearse what to say to the triplets' guardians to make sure she said it with finesse and dignity.

"I didn't know the triplets existed until a few weeks ago. I was grieving so hard that I couldn't handle looking into Angela's personal effects."

Mrs. Romani patted Kristen's hand. "I'm sorry, honey. I

should have been more sensitive. I'm just so used to being tactless with Grant that I sometimes forget not everybody's a pigheaded fool like him."

That made Kristen laugh. "If you dislike the guy so much, why do you work for him?"

"I don't dislike him. I just think he's a man who's far too accustomed to getting his own way." She paused long enough to catch Kristen's gaze. "If you've come here for the kids, you're in for a fight. And you're going to lose. This is *Brewster* County," she said, artificially accenting the Brewster name. "And these guys are *Brewsters*. Because the Brewster lumber mill and the construction project for Grant's new shopping mall employ eighty percent of the population, people fall at their feet to serve them. Especially Grant. Unless the Brewsters were incompetent caretakers, no judge in his right mind would award custody against the wishes of Grant Brewster."

"Are you saying I'm wasting my time?"

"I'm saying you've got to be careful and smart."

Kristen studied the housekeeper. "And if I'm careful and smart, I'll eventually get the kids?"

The housekeeper shook her head. "Those babies are Brewsters. This is their world. This is their empire. Someday *they* will own everything the brothers now control. The best you can hope for is to be part of the kids' lives. And your best bet for being a part of the triplets' lives is to make yourself a place in the lives of the brothers, then explain who you are."

Kristen held the housekeeper's gaze. "I can't do that. These are Morris children every bit as much as they are Brewsters. If I take them back to Texas they'll inherit a multimillion-dollar ranch. If I don't take them back to Texas the ranch will probably go out of my family's hands."

Mrs. Romani sighed and set her rocker in motion. "Okay,

one of two things is going to happen here," she said with
authority. "First, you could tell the Brewsters you need to
take the kids back to Texas to get their ranch, and the
Brewsters will tell you *they* will handle getting the ranch
for the kids." She glanced at Kristen. "Which means *your*
family has as good as lost it. Or, second, you could tell the
Brewsters about your ranch, and they could cooperate with
your plan to take the kids to Texas to get it back into your
family's hands, but they will expect you to bring the kids
home. You're never going to get those kids. Not perma-
nently. And not even for a few months unless the Brewsters
trust you."

"Which way do you think this will pan out?"

"I think you're going to tell them about the ranch. They
will thank you, and then when Chas returns from his honeymoon, he will set the wheels in motion to get the property
for the triplets. Once it's securely in the triplets' hands, it
will be nothing but an investment."

"But that's my home," Kristen protested indignantly.

Mrs. Romani conceded that with a nod. "If you remind
them of that, I'm sure the Brewsters will let you live
there…until they want to sell it."

Obviously seeing the panic-stricken look on Kristen's
face, Mrs. Romani laughed. "Honey, these guys are nothing
if not smart and quick. They won't let the ranch fall out of
the kids' hands, and they might even be sentimental enough
to let you live there, but when push comes to shove, they're
going to handle this like any other business deal."

Absorbing the painful truth, Kristen studied the old
woman. "What about the kids?"

Mrs. Romani looked at her. "What about the kids?"

"I *want* them."

"The Brewsters want them, too."

"But they belong in Texas."

"The Brewsters think they belong in Pennsylvania."

Glancing at her hands, Kristen smiled wryly. "You aren't painting a very nice picture."

"And you aren't taking these kids anywhere," Mrs. Romani said frankly. "Look, honey, I don't think you have much more than a snowball's chance in hell, but just so you get an understanding of how the Brewsters feel about these babies, and also to have a real shot at letting the Brewsters get to know you before they see you as the enemy trying to steal their brother and sisters, I'm going to make a suggestion."

Kristen peeked at her.

"Take the job as the nanny. We'll pretend you're my cousin's daughter who came here this afternoon looking for me, and I'll give you the recommendation you need to get hired."

Kristen shook her head. "I don't think I could do that. It's dishonest."

"Then pack your bags and take yourself back to Texas without these babies. Without getting to *know* these babies," she added emphatically. "Without even really seeing these babies. Because there's no way Grant is going to let you within ten miles of them if he discovers your ultimate goal is to take these kids two thousand miles away."

When Grant opened the door of the nursery and he saw Mrs. Romani and Kristen with their heads bent low in whispered conversation, he knew he hadn't misinterpreted, misrepresented or even misjudged how attractive Kristen was. Her feathery blond hair cascaded around her shoulders, and though her lovely green eyes were intense and serious, they sparkled with warmth. Desire hit him like a punch in the stomach.

Again.

As if he had timed it, Evan slapped him on the back, jolting him back to reality. "So, how are things going up here?"

"Great," Mrs. Romani said, smiling.

"Fine," Kristen said, nodding her head in agreement.

"No problem with the kids?"

"Sleeping like babies," Mrs. Romani said, then laughed at her own joke. "By the way," she added, sliding a quick glance at Kristen. "In all the confusion, we forgot to explain that Kristen is my cousin's daughter. She came here to visit but when I explained that you guys could use some permanent help with the kids, she volunteered. So, if you want her, you've got yourself a nanny."

Grant watched his brother's eyes, widen in surprise. "Hey, that's terrific," Evan said.

But Grant suppressed a sigh of despair. *Wonderful.* This was just wonderful. Now he knew why all his alarm bells went off when he started talking with Kristen. She was related to the woman who couldn't keep a civil tone with him for two sentences even though they lived in the same house and he paid her a damned nice salary. Now he'd have two Romani women in his household. Two women to snip at him and yip at him and yell at him.

"No."

Everybody looked at him.

"No?" Evan echoed stupefied.

"It's never a good policy to have relatives working this closely together," he said, feeling a quick stab of regret when he turned his gaze to Kristen and her beautiful green eyes met his. She was so pretty that he could have happily sighed with pleasure just looking at her. Her pale peaches-and-cream skin invited a touch. He could vividly imagine how wonderful the soft curves of her body would feel pressed against him.

And he knew he didn't want to refuse to hire her because she was Mrs. Romani's cousin's daughter. That was just a convenient excuse. The truth was he didn't want to hire her because he was attracted to her and if she worked for him he would be up against this wicked temptation all day long...twenty-four, seven.

"Look, Grant," Mrs. Romani gruffly commanded. "Kristen needs this job. Could you put your feelings aside for a few weeks and let her show you that she can be a good nanny?"

Fighting a grimace, Grant recognized Mrs. Romani didn't know how close to the truth she was. Could he put his feelings aside for a few weeks?

As a gentleman, and a man who also desperately needed help with his three kids, he had to.

"Then if she doesn't work out," Mrs. Romani continued as Grant dragged himself out of his thoughts and back into the real world, "she'll leave and you can find somebody else."

"She can stay," Grant said, trying not to sound magnanimous and sanctimonious, and subduing his own apprehension. He couldn't do anything about the fact that Kristen was ravishing, but he could conquer the vulnerability and yearnings that sprung up watching Chas get married. And he would, damn it, he *would*.

Unfortunately even as he said the words that granted his permission, he realized that since Mrs. Romani had the maid's quarters on the first floor, this woman to whom he found himself unreasonably attracted would now be sleeping two doors down the hall.

Before he strode out of the room, he thanked God they didn't have to share a bathroom. If he caught her in the bathtub, surrounded by bubbles...

Well, he just didn't want to go there.

Chapter Two

After the wedding guests had gone, Mrs. Romani showed Kristen to her room, and Kristen took the opportunity to change out of her dress and into jeans and a sweater. When she returned downstairs, she discovered the triplets had been fed a light snack. But before she panicked about not knowing what a nanny should be doing, Grant announced it was time to take the girls upstairs and get them ready for bed.

Kristen climbed the elegant spiral stairway behind Grant, Evan and Claire, the bridesmaid in the autumn-orange dress who Kristen learned was Evan's wife. She wasn't exactly sure why it took four people to dress two babies for bed, and she was even more confused about why they weren't getting Cody ready for bed, but she also wasn't about to question anything. The less she said, the better. Since caring for babies was supposed to come naturally, she didn't think the Brewsters would notice her lack of experience with kids as long as she kept her wits about her, but one out-of-place question or comment could give her away.

When she realized how crafty and cautious she would

have to be to keep this charade going, she wondered if Mrs. Romani's plan was the best way to handle integrating herself into the Brewster family. Though her intentions were good, she also knew what she was doing wasn't honest. Unfortunately now that the wheels were in motion, she was stuck. Until she ingratiated herself to these people, revealing who she was could actually backfire and make it look like she was nothing more than a liar and a sneak. She had to stick this out for as long as it took to show them she was a good person, not someone prone to charades, trickery and lying.

Grant opened the nursery door and Evan and Claire followed him into the rainbow strewn room. Nervous, and out of her element, Kristen hung behind.

"Isn't this a lovely nursery?" Claire said as she walked over to Kristen and casually slid one of the children into her arms, apparently thinking Kristen wouldn't be so bold as to do something without permission. "This is Annie. She's Chas's child."

Feeling the softness of the baby's skin, smelling the sweet scent of baby powder, and looking into green eyes exactly like Angela's, Kristen felt emotions so strong and so deep she struggled to control them. She cleared her throat, and focused her attention on what Claire had said. "Chas's child?" she asked quietly.

Evan swung the little boy off the changing table and playfully tossed him to Claire, as he said, "Claire, here, came up with the bright idea that we'd need to do something a little out of the ordinary to make sure each child got special attention. So, we each took responsibility for one child. Cody is ours," he said, pointing to the little boy Claire held. "Responsibility for Annie belongs to Chas, and Grant cares for Taylor," he added, nodding toward the dark-haired little girl sitting on Grant's lap.

When she looked at the beautiful baby, Kristen wondered how her fair-haired, pale-skinned sister could have had a child so dark, then her gaze collided with that of Grant and Kristen didn't have to think any further. Taylor didn't merely have Morris blood, she also shared blood with Grant—and right now Grant was their primary guardian. If Kristen wanted these kids, her fight was with him. From the wary look on his face, Kristen could almost believe that was the message he was sending her with his smoky, watchful eyes.

Except he didn't know she was Taylor's aunt. Which meant the expression was intended to convey something entirely different. The same thing he'd been inadvertently communicating all afternoon. The same thing she'd sensed ten seconds after he opened his door to her. They were attracted to each other. And because of her choice they were now living together. Obviously the situation didn't please him.

If they behaved like mature, honorable adults, it wouldn't be a problem, Kristen thought and glanced away. For her it was a no-brainer, not something she had to ponder or brood about.

Besides, she wasn't worried about the attraction anymore. All she had to do was remember Bradley, how much she adored him, how hard it was to lose him, how raw the wounds of deprivation could be when you lost someone you cherished, and no man could be attractive to her anymore.

"Do you want me to stay and help show Kristen the ropes?" Claire asked Grant, bringing Kristen back to the matter at hand.

Grant caught Kristen's gaze again. "No. You guys grab Cody and head on home. It's been a long day for all of us. I'm sure Kristen and I can handle things alone."

Kristen quickly, easily got the point of what he was telling her with his black, black eyes. He'd bided his time wait-ing for wedding guests to leave, waiting for Mrs. Romani to show Kristen to her room, and allowing Kristen a few minutes to change into comfortable clothes, but as soon as Claire and Evan left, he and Kristen would have a heart-to-heart chat. Since he hadn't been able to get out of hiring her, he probably had every intention of laying down the law.

But it appeared that Evan and his wife were oblivious to the firmness of Grant's voice because Evan said, "You know, Grant, there's something I needed to discuss with you. Dad had an investment in the pension fund that doesn't look right to me. If you'd give me ten minutes to run over the paperwork with you, you could study it and give me your opinion. If you agree with me, I'd like to sell this dog before the end of the month."

As Evan and his wife walked to the nursery door, Grant cast a skeptical eye toward Kristen. "Can you handle both girls by yourself for a minute?"

Though her heart thumped wildly at the prospect of being *alone* with the babies, Kristen shrugged casually, "Yeah. Sure. Why not?"

Still cautious, Grant placed Taylor into the play yard and headed toward the door. Claire turned and, with Cody's hand, waved goodbye to Kristen and the girls, and the Brewsters exited, leaving Kristen behind with her two nieces and the echoing silence.

Glad that Grant had given her time to change into blue jeans and a sweater, Kristen sat Annie on the nursery floor, then reached into the play yard, pulled out Taylor and sat her beside her sister.

Leaning back on her haunches, Kristen stared at them. The girls were dressed in two-piece yellow pajamas with plastic-bottomed feet. Like a little lady, Taylor sat primly and smiled at Kristen. Annie, however, began to howl.

"Shh!" Kristen said quickly, afraid Grant would hear and return before she had a chance to get acquainted with the babies. She scooped Annie off the floor with one arm while reaching for Taylor with the other. "Darn it, Annie, you look so much like your mother, couldn't you have been born with her sweet, sweet disposition? Did you have to turn out like me?"

As if actually understanding what had been said, Annie stopped wailing and peered at Kristen.

"Yes. That's right. We share a gene pool. I'm your mother's sister. There's a very good possibility you could turn out exactly like me—except looking like your mother."

This time, Taylor cocked her head and studied Kristen.

"And you," she said to Taylor. "You look so doggone much like your half brother that it scares me. But at least you act like your mother."

As if fully comprehending the discussion and happy at the prospect of being like her mother, Taylor smiled, then squealed with glee as she clapped her chubby little hands.

Kristen's heart lurched. She squeezed her eyes shut to gather her wits before walking to the first available rocker. She felt like fate was reminding her that these kids knew nothing about their mother and would never know about their mother. She doubted the Brewsters could tell the children much since Angela hadn't been in their family for very long.

Snuggling both girls against her, Kristen leaned back on the rocker. She hadn't known about these children until she received a letter from Angela's lawyer announcing that he was withdrawing as counsel in Angela's claim for the Morris family ranch. Holding the girls close, Kirsten experienced strange, compelling feelings. These babies weren't merely all she had left, they could easily become the meaning and purpose for her existence. After her husband Bradley's death, her life was nothing more than day-to-day emptiness, but with the knowledge that she needed to be the mother to her sister's three children, something wonderful had been born in her. More than a reason to live, a reason to be happy. A reason to rejoice.

But custody of the kids belonged to men she didn't even know in a state two thousand miles away from her home. They were rich, they were powerful, and she only owned the clothes on her back.

The fight, if it came down to that, would not be a fair one, and she understood why Mrs. Romani had suggested Kristen demonstrate to this family that she was a good, kind, generous person before she not only revealed who she was but also announced that she needed to take these children to Texas.

At the sound of the nursery doorknob turning, signaling Grant's return, Kristen became fully alert. One swift frown got the attention of the squirming babies on her lap. "Things are strained enough between us already," she quickly whispered. "If your brother thinks you're misbehaving for me, he might ask me to leave."

Though she thought her rationalization explained everything sufficiently that the girls would obey, Taylor then let out with a squeal and immediately thereafter Annie followed suit. "*Shh!*" she admonished quietly.

"Don't waste your breath," Grant said, closing the door behind him. "They're wound-up from all the attention at the wedding. But more than that, they won't listen to you because you're new."

He added the last as he scooped Taylor from Kristen's lap. In one smooth motion, he raised her above his head, then swung her down far enough that he could blow on her belly. The action caused Taylor to squeal.

Terrified for the baby's safety, Kristen gaped at him. "What the heck is that?"

"It's called playing," Grant replied, then swung Taylor over his head again.

Kristen bounced from her seat ready to rescue the little girl, but when she realized Taylor was squealing with delight, not fright, she stopped dead in her tracks. "She likes that?"

Grant cast a curious glance at Kristen. "She *expects* this from me."

"She *expects* to be roughhoused?"

"She expects to be *played with*," Grant corrected with a laugh, then shifted the little girl into the crook of his arm and reached into the small refrigerator in the corner of the room and pulled out a baby bottle. He tossed it to Kristen.

Only through the grace of God and good reflexes did she catch it.

"Feed Annie."

She looked at the bottle, then the baby, then back at Grant again. But preoccupied with grabbing another bottle, kicking the refrigerator door closed and carrying Taylor to a rocker, he didn't seem to see that she didn't know what to do.

As he sat, Kristen saw that he noticed she hadn't moved and he sighed heavily. "Slide the nipple into her mouth," he suggested evenly.

"I was just a little shell-shocked from having a bottle tossed at me," Kristen said, trying to cover for the fact that she'd never given a baby a bottle before. She'd *seen* mothers feed babies, dress them, diaper them. She watched all her friends have children and begin to raise them, but she hadn't actually *done* any of the baby work with or for them.

"Whatever," Grant said, sliding the nipple of the bottle into Taylor's mouth, then relaxing against the back of his rocker. Without another word, he closed his eyes.

Because she'd been primed for a fight or a lecture, Kristen frowned as she gave the bottle to Annie and got comfortable in her rocker. Confused, but guessing that Grant's brother might have cautioned him against saying anything that might lose their "nanny," she covertly studied Grant.

Eyes closed, wearing jeans and a sweatshirt, and restfully lounging in the rocker, he was casually gorgeous, but also the epitome of a well-practiced dad. *He* could have been the babies' father. In fact, he *should have been* the triplet's father. Somewhere in his mid-thirties, Grant was probably closer to Angela's age than Norm Brewster had been.

Remembering her own shock at being told in Arnie Garrett's letter that Angela had had triplets with someone from a different generation, Kristen couldn't even speculate on the Brewster brothers' reaction. How would the grown children of an elderly man take the news that they had infant siblings? Surely they didn't rejoice. Second families were always a little hard to take and with the addition of more people into this particular bloodline, the Brewsters would also have to share their inheritance. Nine chances out of ten, they'd been angry with their father—probably furious—when these children were born. And now they were forced to raise the same kids whose very existence had cut their net worths in half.

"Do you resent these kids?" she blurted into the quiet room, too appalled that the Brewsters might mistreat the babies to think clearly, but simultaneously regretting being nosy. Recognizing she had to somehow cover that slip, she added, "Your father must have married a woman a lot younger than he was to have babies. So, you couldn't have been happy."

Still not opening his eyes, Grant said, "Mrs. Romani filled your head with the village gossip, I see."

"She didn't say anything," Kristen said, then paused, realizing it was true. The only thing that had really concerned Mrs. Romani was that Kristen understood Grant Brewster wasn't an easy man to get along with. From his blunt assumption, she was beginning to see why. "I'm just curious."

"All right," he said. Sighing heavily, he opened his eyes and faced her, never once jostling or disturbing the baby he was feeding. "You're going to hear it eventually anyway, so I'll tell you that I wasn't pleased when my father remarried two months after my mother died. I threw a fit, left town, dragged my brothers with me and didn't return until my father died."

Kristen heard the remorse that resonated through the last part, the part about his father, and she felt guilty for asking. Obviously Norm had married Angela to help the Morris family regain control of their ranch. If he hadn't explained that to his sons, though, it sounded as if that was because they hadn't given him a chance.

Unfortunately she also couldn't explain to Grant Brewster that his father had married her sister because the Morrises were about to lose their family home. When her father and uncle were killed together in an airplane accident, the property reverted to a childless aunt, who didn't know how to bequeath it. So, in her will she'd stipulated that the first Morris to have a child inherited the ranch, provided he or she agreed to live there with that child. But when Aunt Paige died, Morrises came out of the woodwork, each claiming he was the rightful heir, forcing Angela, Kristen and a handful of California relatives to prove they were the only people with a direct line to the property.

But one of them still had to have a child to claim it. If Norm Brewster married her sister and immediately made her pregnant, Kristen could only assume he'd done it as a kindness.

She couldn't reveal all this to Grant Brewster because if she went into that kind of detail with him, no matter how speculatively, she would give herself away. But she would explain. Soon. And when she did, Grant Brewster could forgive himself.

"I'm sorry I asked," Kristen said, intending to change the subject. "It's really none of my business."

"No, it's fine," Grant insisted coolly. "This is a conversation we needed to get out of the way. It is unusual for grown men to have baby siblings. If you were curious, I can understand why."

The quiet tone of his voice filled her with compassion. She could tell that beneath his very calm, composed demeanor was a suffering man. Sensitive to his need for comforting in a way she'd never been with anyone before, she nestled Annie closer as she said, "If it's any consolation, I know a thing or two about loss."

She hesitated, torn, but decided she owed Grant something since she reopened wounds better left closed. If nothing else she could let him know he wasn't alone in the world. "My husband died a little over a year ago, my sister a few months later."

He glanced at her. "I'm sorry. My parents died two years apart, so I had some time to adjust. Your situation must have been terrible."

"It was," Kristen said, suddenly realizing how desperate she was to talk with someone who would understand the way she knew this man would understand. But talking about Angela with a Brewster would be courting trouble and discussing losing her husband was still too painful, too personal to discuss.

"But everybody has his or her cross to bear."

Grant nodded. "Funny how we thought these kids were

going to be something like a cross to bear and they ended up being the best thing that ever happened to us.''

Smiling softly as she looked at the big, dark man cuddling the tiny child, Kristen nodded. "I can see that."

"So that must be why you came looking for Mrs. Romani?" Grant asked, still gazing at his suckling baby.

Kristen's brow puckered. "Excuse me?"

"Losing your sister and your husband must have been what prompted you to come looking for Mrs. Romani."

Catching on to what he was saying, Kristen let the sentence swirl around in her head long enough for her to realize half of it was true—or the essence of it was true—and it didn't complicate things to admit it. "Yes. It was my sister's death that brought me here," she said carefully.

"So you're not close to Mrs. Romani?" Grant asked.

She shook her head. "No, we're not close at all."

He caught her gaze. "She didn't raise you or anything like that?"

This time Kristen giggled. "No, Mr. Worrywart, she did not raise me."

If anyone else had laughed at him and called him Mr. Worrywart, Grant would have definitely taken offense. Since it was Kristen, and since they were cuddling babies and sharing their very private, painful backgrounds with each other, Grant not only didn't take offense, but he actually chuckled.

"I'm sorry, but my dislike for Mrs. Romani is such common knowledge around here that I sometimes forget most normal people don't behave like this."

"Why don't you like her?"

Grant considered that. "It isn't so much that I don't like her. It's more that she has an annoying habit of trying to control everything or run everybody's life, or something."

"She said approximately the same thing about you."

He peered at her. "Really?"

"Yeah, she said you like to be the boss, you try to run everybody's life and you always have to have your own way. So, she confronts you to more or less keep everything balanced."

"Really?" he asked curiously.

"She doesn't dislike you. I think she sees her belligerence as more self-defense than anything else. She doesn't want to get swept up in the tidal wave. She sees you as being very...powerful, and not afraid to use that power."

Carefully maneuvering the baby he held, Grant freed his right hand so he could rub it across the back of his neck. He didn't know why it felt so good or so right to talk with this woman—actually, to confide in her as he'd never confided to anyone in his life—but it did. And he was too tired to fight it.

"I'm responsible for the lives of three babies, two brothers and now the wives of two brothers. We own the mill that employs fifty percent of the people in this county, and I'm putting in a shopping mall that will employ another thirty percent when it's up and running. If all goes well, my construction company will pick up everybody who is left and even some people from surrounding counties. I don't have time to stop and consider everybody's feelings and everybody's opinion."

"Maybe you should."

He stared at her. "How?" he asked incredulously. "Should I take a Gallop poll?"

She laughed at him again and his eyes narrowed. He should be angry with her for laughing at him. Instead he felt only breathless relief that he could actually talk about his burdens with an objective, independent listener.

"No, but you could try looking around every once in a

while. Check for a grimace or a frown. Ask your brothers for an opinion here and there.''

"I *do* ask for my brothers' opinions."

"Do you take them into consideration?"

"Of course, I take…" He stopped. He honestly didn't really know if he ever took his brothers' opinions into consideration. He listened to them, then tossed them into the vat of information stored in his brain, which he assimilated in a certain fashion, then used to make decisions as he needed them.

"You don't know, do you?" Kristen asked archly.

He rubbed his hand across the back of his neck again. What was he doing, confiding in a stranger? Yes, he knew it felt good to have somebody to talk with, especially someone objective, but this woman was only objective because she was a newcomer to his household. She was also an employee. No smart boss confided in his employees.

"No, I don't know," he replied. "And this conversation is over."

"Can't handle it?"

"No. It's none of your business," Grant corrected, rising and walking to a crib. "I've known you eight hours and I've already told you my deepest, darkest secrets."

Following suit, Kristen also took her baby to a crib. "If those were your deepest, darkest secrets, Grant Brewster, you've got to get a life."

The words sent an odd chill up Grant's spine because they were exactly the thoughts he'd been having as he watched his baby brother get married.

Careful, cautious, he faced her. In her little pink sweater and a pair of loose-fitting jeans that knew exactly which parts of her anatomy to hug, Kristen Devereaux didn't have a clue how much he really wanted to have a life—or at least some good old-fashioned excitement—with her.

Kristen seemed too damned young to have been married. She seemed too damned young not to have any family but a cantankerous old bat housekeeper she didn't know. She seemed too damned young to be wise, and wonderful…and widowed.

Actually she was probably too damned young for him.

He took a long breath and blew it out. "Let's go," he said, motioning to the door. "Though the triplets usually sleep through the night now, there are no guarantees. There's a monitor in your room and one in mine. First one to awaken has to get the kids. That's the rule. So, I suggest that you go straight to your room and go straight to bed."

Boy, he wished he hadn't said that. Instant, graphic images of her sliding between satin sheets came to mind. He could see her hair fanned out on a pillow. He could envision her face softened in sleep. He could *feel* her nestled against him.

Oh, great! As if he needed to remind himself of the last image.

"Because that's exactly what I'm going to do. I'm going to shower—" *in cold water* "—and then I'm going straight to bed."

He said the last as he led her into the hall and more or less pointed her to the bedroom she'd been assigned.

But as he shuffled off as if his feet were on fire, Kristen dallied in going to her room. When she heard his door shut with a very distinct and final click, she pivoted and ran down the hall, down the steps of the spiral staircase, through the foyer and kitchen and to Mrs. Romani's door.

It opened immediately.

"Well?" the gruff-voiced housekeeper asked as she granted Kristen entry.

"I think everything went okay. But I didn't actually make up a story like you told me to. We started talking and before

I knew it I was explaining that my husband and sister had died.''

Mrs. Romani gasped in horror.

''I didn't go into any kind of detail and he assumed that because my family had died I'd come looking for a long, lost relative—you.''

''*He* came up with that?''

Kristen nodded.

Mrs. Romani grinned. ''Oh, that's rich.''

But Kristen frowned. ''I don't like fooling him. I don't like fooling anybody.''

''That's why this is so rich,'' Mrs. Romani said, patting Kristen's hand. ''*You* never told him anything. He made assumptions. Now we don't have to make up a story. We can more or less behave like strangers getting to know each other, which we are. And we also don't have to worry that he'll ask too many questions because you told him you lost your family, and he's very sensitive about loss.''

Kristen licked her suddenly dry lips. ''I know.''

''He *confided* in you?''

''Little things. Bits and pieces,'' Kristen clarifed uncertainly.

''Well, now,'' Mrs. Romani said, and with a satisfied smirk directed Kristen to the door. ''Sounds like everything will run smooth as clockwork. I don't have anything to worry about. And you don't have anything to worry about.''

But she did, Kristen thought, sneaking back to her room. She wasn't a person who was built for deception, and she especially didn't like deceiving someone as burdened as Grant Brewster. But more than that, they had feelings for each other. Not only were they instantly attracted, but they were instantly empathetic, because they'd gone through some similar situations. When he discovered who she was he was going to be insulted and angry, unless she kept their relationship distant or, if possible, nonexistent from this point forward so his level of betrayal would be lower than it would be if they became friends.

Since that was the logical choice, that's what she intended to do. Keep her distance. Avoid becoming friends. Ignore the attraction.

Chapter Three

Kristen had the girls dressed in bright pink sweat suits and was feeding them breakfast when Grant came downstairs the next morning. Everything was under control until she looked up at the kitchen doorway in which he stood, then the spoon she held stopped midway to Taylor's open mouth.

Not only was he wearing a neat black suit, white shirt and paisley tie, but he had shaved his beard. *His beard.* The one thing about him that could be construed as even remotely unattractive was gone. Replaced by a clean, smooth face of angles and planes so handsome and male that Kristen's heart skipped a beat.

He caught her gaze and gave her a casual smile, but Kristen only stared at him.

"Good morning," he said and walked into the room. "I saw that you had the kids up so I just got myself dressed. I hope it wasn't a problem."

"The children got me up about an hour ago," Kristen said as she slid a spoonful of oatmeal into Annie's mouth. Shaving his beard had taken her by surprise, but her reaction to him wasn't new. The night before she'd decided to handle this, and she would. "Mrs. Romani helped me with breakfast."

"I helped her *prepare* breakfast," Mrs. Romani corrected, because—Grant knew—his short housekeeper with the overbleached hair and a sharp, crackly voice from cigarettes had no intention of letting anyone get the wrong impression. "As far as those babies go, she's handled everything herself."

"Really?" Grant asked, striding to the coffeepot, sternly stifling the tingles of awareness that were beginning to expand in his stomach. With Kristen's sleep-tousled hair, and her curves clearly outlined by the soft flannel of her yellow robe, not only did she look cuddly and beautiful, but her genuine interest in the babies gave her an allure that couldn't be matched by mere physical beauty.

But though the tingles of awareness yearned to turn into full-scale sexual arousal, Grant was determined not to let them. Kristen Devereaux was a woman with problems. He might not have clearly realized that the night before, but in the light of day everything had made perfect sense. She understood him because she understood loss. He was grieving his father, regretting his mistakes. She was grieving her husband and her sister. They were an emotionally wounded duo, who definitely, positively, absolutely shouldn't get involved.

But beyond that, he wasn't *allowed* to get involved with her. She was an employee. The complications that could result from the two of them becoming personal were too numerous to mention and too serious to be ignored. A wise man stayed the hell away from his employees. Period.

"Since Cody's with Claire and Evan, there were only two babies for me to dress and feed," Kristen said, bringing Grant back to the present as she set Annie's spoon down and reached for Taylor's. "Besides, the girls are sweet and well behaved."

At that Grant involuntarily chuckled, but when Kristen gave him a puzzled frown he stopped laughing. "I'm sorry, I thought you were kidding."

"Kidding?"

He shrugged. "Annie and Taylor are trouble with a capital *T*. Annie by herself is as lovable as a kitten. Alone, Taylor is a little lady. But put them together and they are holy terrors."

"No, they aren't," Kristen objected, continuing to feed the kids.

Grant turned to Mrs. Romani. "Is she serious?"

Mrs. Romani tossed her hands as if exasperated to be brought into the discussion, but she said, "I haven't ever seen the girls so quiet."

"Well, I'll be damned," Grant said and walked over to the table in the breakfast nook. From the way Kristen seemed hesitant with the girls the night before, he wouldn't have guessed her capable of taking care of the morning routine alone. He sat on the captain's chair beside Kristen's, leaning in to get a good view of what she was doing. Not only was she handling things much better than Grant would have guessed her able, but the girls had *never* been this well mannered. If there was a lesson to be learned here, he was willing to learn it.

"See?" Kristen said, spooning more oatmeal into Annie's mouth. Like an angel, Annie obediently opened and closed her lips when required, while Taylor sat patiently, waiting for her turn.

Grant stared at them. "Amazing. How do you do that?"

"I don't know," Kristen said, but Grant noticed a blush stain her cheeks and he seriously wondered if she hadn't done something this morning to get the girls to behave. If they were older he'd think she'd bribed them with a present.

Incredulous, Grant bent in closer. "Taylor, honey, don't you want to put your bowl on your head and wear it like a hat?"

Taylor cocked her head and gave him a look as if to say she would never do something so naughty.

"Annie? No scream?"

Annie only giggled.

Mrs. Romani shook her head in bewilderment. "I'm telling you. She's a miracle worker."

"I am not," Kristen objected, almost too vehemently.

Grant had his suspicions about how she'd gotten the children to be good, but he didn't care if she had bribed them. As long as they were safe and happy, he wasn't questioning anything.

"I think you're a miracle worker," Grant said, laying his arm across the back of her chair and finding himself in intimate proximity. Not only was he close enough to touch her, but those last three inches put him in the direct line of seeing her smooth, shiny hair up close. He also caught a whiff of her scent. A flowery bouquet hit him so unexpectedly, he didn't stop himself from catching it.

The soft fragrance brought him spontaneous ecstasy and he automatically inhaled again. But he rationalized that he still didn't have anything to worry about. So what if he'd inadvertently lingered over that scent a little longer than he should have? It didn't mean anything. He had his perspective firmly grounded. He had no intention of getting involved with this woman. He simply had enjoyed her cologne. No big deal. In fact, he wouldn't mind another whiff. As silently as possible, he sniffed the air, then narrowed his eyes in pleasure.

"Well, good morning, Grant," Evan said, stepping into the room, carrying Cody.

Caught red-handed, Grant leaped out of the chair. "Evan!" he said, realizing too late that the move made him look even more guilty.

Evan gasped. "You shaved!"

Grant nonchalantly rubbed his clean chin. "I was tired of the beard."

Big-eyed and incredulous, Evan grinned. "Really?"

"Really." Grant mimicked, his eyes narrowing in warning.

Still grinning, Evan strolled a little farther into the kitchen. "Looks like you and Kristen are getting along very well...with the children."

Though everyone else in the room appeared oblivious, Grant recognized that Evan had added enough of a pause in his statement to get in a pointed, inappropriate jab of teasing.

Mature, proper, Grant chose not to rise to the bait. He even knew how to nip his brother's misconception in the bud. "Actually Kristen's handled everything herself. I was just trying to figure out what she'd done to get the kids to behave so well this morning."

"I could see that," Evan agreed, the teasing still in his voice, and his eyes bright with the joy of tormenting his older brother. "The way you were leaning right in there, so close to Kristen...and the girls," he said, again adding the second part of the statement after another significant pause. "I could see that you were trying to...figure out Kristen's secrets."

Grant glared at his brother. His first instinct was to call Evan a moron. Instead he picked up his coffee cup, gulped down the steamy liquid and strode toward the back door. For the love of God, the woman was young enough to be his...sister. Sister. Not daughter. He refused to say daughter. Refused. He wasn't that old. Only thirty-six. And she had to be at least twenty-three. Maybe even twenty-four or twenty-five. To have been married and widowed, Kristen could even be a year or two older. She acted older. She *looked* older. Hell, she looked at least twenty-five....

He stopped himself. *Was he arguing for or against her?*

"And, really, Grant, you're so much more attractive without the beard," Evan said, still teasing. "Though I have to wonder why you didn't shave for Chas's wedding. That would have made more sense than waiting until after the ceremony and the pictures and everything. I wonder what could have happened since the wedding to change your mind."

The more Evan needled him, the more obvious and idiotic Grant felt. If his brother had noticed the way he was carrying on, and deduced why Grant had shaved, then the only person Grant was fooling was himself. He needed to somehow regain his perspective, and he had to behave when he was forced to be around Kristen instead of letting unruly, hormone-driven instincts take over. No more confidence sharing. No more dressing to look better because she was around. And definitely no more sniffing the air.

He grabbed the doorknob. "I have meetings until noon, and I don't think I can be back to help with lunch. Mrs. Romani, I want pot roast for supper."

"Yes, sir," Mrs. Romani said, saluting him as he stormed out of the door.

Kristen breathed a sigh of relief that he was gone, then rose and reached for Cody. "Hello, honey," she cooed sweetly to the little boy.

He peered at her, his face puckered into a scowl, and before Kristen realized what was happening he began to cry.

"Oh, oh," Evan said, taking Cody back again. "I think he's making strange."

"Making strange?" Kristen asked, alarmed that her own nephew wouldn't like her, though she realized the poor kid couldn't like someone he didn't know.

"We spoil him," Evan admitted with a grimace.

"There's an understatement," Mrs. Romani said, laughing as she began tidying up the kitchen.

Cody continued to cry and within seconds had both of his sisters wailing with him.

"There goes your run of good luck," Mrs. Romani said wryly.

"As long as Grant didn't see them, I don't care," Kristen said without thinking. She forgot Evan was as much of a consideration as Grant until the words were already out of her mouth. Stumbling to recover, she added, "Once I start playing with them, I'm sure they'll be fine."

Evan gave her a sympathetic look. "Not when they're this wound up," he said amiably, as if dealing with the kids was second nature to him and not something that got him flustered or frazzled. "I'll call Claire and see if she can rearrange our schedules so that one or both of us can stay with you this morning."

Kristen peeked at Mrs. Romani.

Mrs. Romani subtly nodded her endorsement that Kristen could take the offer without fear of reprisal.

The breath she was holding burst out in a whoosh. "You mean it?"

"Of course," Evan said, walking to the wall phone by the door. Juggling Cody and dialing simultaneously, he added, "We're all trying to work together here, but Grant's the one with the most input. If he doesn't like the way you're handling the kids, he won't keep you."

Kristen smiled with sardonic acknowledgment. "I figured that out for myself."

"Not a problem. We'll teach you the ropes," Evan said, dismissing the whole business as if it were no big deal. "Before this is all over, Claire and I will turn you into a professional."

"You'd do that for me?"

He shrugged. "You and the kids."

A wave of gratitude washed over Kristen until she realized what had just happened. Not only had she let down her guard with one of the brothers, but that same brother had put the health, safety and well-being of the triplets ahead of his business.

Kristen stopped that line of thought because that wasn't precisely what he had done as much as it was her *interpretation* of what he'd done.

Besides, she wasn't here to make any determinations about the Brewsters, whether or not they were good caretakers or whether or not she should feel guilty about wanting to get custody of the triplets. She was here to prove herself. Even if the only thing she could get from these men was the opportunity to take the kids to Texas long enough to get the ranch, she still had to prove to them that she was capable of handling three babies for the time they would be in her custody.

If anything, she'd just scored a strike against herself.

Dinner with the Brewster triplets was an adventure.

Though Claire had stayed with Kristen through the morning, and even helped with lunch, she needed to get back to the lumber mill and left Kristen alone to handle the afternoon by herself. Given that the children typically took a long nap, neither Kristen nor Claire felt there would be a problem, but the kids didn't seem to want to sleep.

They wanted to play. And cry. And play. And cry. Because Kristen wasn't sure if she should let them cry themselves to sleep, or play with them until they were exhausted, she tried a little of both and the result was that she confused them. Eventually all three children fell asleep, but none of them slept more than twenty minutes.

Since they hadn't napped as long as they needed, they were exhausted by the time dinner rolled around, and all three were cranky and restless. The girls were so bad Evan and Claire took one look at them and knew Kristen couldn't feed them alone.

So they stayed and helped with dinner, again giving Kristen the awkward feeling that she wasn't moving forward, but losing points. But since the brother who saw was Evan, not Grant, she wasn't ready to panic yet. She didn't know where Grant was, but she did know she was grateful he hadn't seen the three-ring circus they called dinner.

When Grant finally did arrive home, all her fears about him evaporated. He liked her. She saw it the second their eyes met. She knew he'd stormed out of the house that morning because his brother was teasing him, but his annoyance was a confirmation to Kristen that he planned to dismiss their attraction the same way she did. Unfortunately his ignoring the attraction could also have the backlash that he would be cautious about getting along with her. She had to get him to see that instantly accepting her, even liking her, wasn't a problem, particularly now that their sexual attraction was under control. She had to bring him back to where they were the night before. Confiding in and appreciating each other without weeks and weeks of getting acquainted.

Because they didn't have weeks and weeks to spend getting acquainted. Everybody would be angry if she took too long before admitting who she was, but she figured out that morning that no one would blame her for taking a week or two to get comfortable with them before revealing her identity. So she couldn't waste time while Grant grumbled and blustered around the house pretending he didn't like her or hadn't yet approved of her. No matter what it took, she would push him to treat her normally, to be relaxed with her, and even to admit out loud, among friends and family, that he liked her.

By the time she was done with him, he would not only trust her with his life, but he would publicly acknowledge that.

And the beauty of it was she didn't have to fake or fudge or even pretend to be something she wasn't. All she had to do was be herself, to build on what they'd started the night before, and eventually he would be so comfortable he wouldn't treat her any differently when they were with other people than when they were alone.

Evan and Claire kissed the girls goodbye, bundled Cody into his one-piece wool outerwear and were gone before Kristen even had time to properly thank them for everything they had done that day, but it almost didn't matter. Grant Brewster was her main concern. He had to be. Not only was he lord and master of the Brewster empire, but he also liked her. She'd heard it in his voice the night before and saw it in the way he looked at her that morning. She refused to let him get away with pretending otherwise just because it was good for his image.

"How was work today?" she asked, making small talk while they undressed the girls for their baths. The first part of her plan was to remind him that he had no trouble talking with her. When she admitted who she was she didn't want it to be a strained, stilted conversation, so it couldn't be unusual that they talked. By the time she made her confession, she wanted Grant so accustomed to having private conversations with her that when she sat him down to have the discussion that mattered the most he would be comfortable, congenial.

"It was fine," he mumbled, clearly not in the mood for casual conversation. He rolled Taylor off the changing table and strode away from Kristen, into the bathroom.

Kristen quickly grabbed Annie and scrambled into the bathroom behind Grant. "We had a great day, here," she said, shifting the topic to her and the kids. Since it was his responsibility to hear how things had gone with the kids, it was the perfect way to keep the friendly mood they had last night and when he first arrived in the kitchen this morning. "Claire actually spent a good bit of time with us. Helping me get adjusted," she admitted, sliding Annie into the tub with her sister. If the subject ever came up in a conversation between Grant and Claire, Kristen didn't want him to think she'd tried to hide it. "She's a wonderful person."

Swishing his hand through the warm water to make suds for the kids, Grant grunted an acknowledgment, but didn't look at her.

Kristen refused to be daunted. "She tells me her mother had a second family when she was in high school and that's how she learned to care for babies."

Grant sighed. "It's not a secret."

"Obviously," Kristen agreed, struggling for another bit of small talk to keep the conversation going. As if sensing that the adults were having a hard time, Annie squealed and splashed her hands in the water. "Oh, you love the water, don't you, honey?" Kristen said, palming a handful of suds and blowing them in the air above the babies' heads.

Annie squealed, Taylor giggled.

"I'll get fresh towels," Grant mumbled and strode away. Falling back on her haunches, Kristen sighed. Annie smiled at her, but Taylor cocked her head as if trying to figure out what was wrong.

"Your brother can be a real pain in the butt," she whispered, leaning forward to speak directly to Taylor.

Taylor giggled again.

"Is he always this grouchy and hard to talk to?"

As Kirsten soaped and cleaned the babies' tiny bodies, one clear thought overrode her concerns about Grant. These girls were beautiful, wonderful, soft reminders of her sister, but they were also little people in their own right. She loved these kids and she would regret it if she spent all her time immersed in Grant Brewster's feelings for her and didn't savor the precious opportunity she had with them.

She suspected that was what Annie had been trying to tell her when she splashed the water, and maybe even what Grant had been trying to tell her with his silence. He wanted this time to enjoy the kids, not listen to her chatter.

When Grant brought the fresh towels into the room, she warmly wrapped Annie in the soft terry cloth and took her to the changing table. A few seconds later, Grant joined her cooing and cuddling Taylor.

His ability with the kids never ceased to amaze her— particularly since he took such pride in being gruff with everyone else. Watching him with the girls was like watching an entirely different person.

"You're very good with the kids," she complimented softly, fully expecting him to ignore her again.

But Grant surprised her by smiling and saying, "Claire had to teach me and my brothers how to hold the kids and even how to show them affection because we'd never even been around a baby."

The emotion shimmering through his words filled Kristen's heart with pleasure. "Well, you're very good with them now."

"Thank you," Grant said, then carrying Taylor, strode to the refrigerator. He got a bottle and went to the rocker.

After snapping the last snap of Annie's pajamas, Kristen followed suit. As Grant had done only a minute or so before her, she got a bottle, took a seat on a rocker and began to feed her baby.

"Even with coaching from Claire we still had a hard time getting adjusted to being parents," Grant whispered into the silence of the semidark nursery. "I know these kids are just normal, healthy babies, but when you multiply any child's behavior by three you end up with a ton of trouble."

"Tell me about it," Kristen agreed, rocking Annie as she remembered their less than stellar afternoon. "Many times today I felt like I needed to be in three places at once."

"Well, it won't be like this much longer. We were so accustomed to how well Lily took care of the kids that we forgot you're new. I spoke with Evan this morning and he'd like to work out some kind of schedule wherein we divide the duties so that each of us spends a certain amount of time here until you get settled."

"That's more or less what Claire and Evan did today," Kristen admitted, glad that she'd already mentioned getting Claire's help.

Because he felt oddly guilty for being cool with her even though he knew it was the right thing to do, but more because he didn't want her to get the impression that he was angry with her for not being able to handle the kids alone, Grant sighed. "You're doing fine," he said, trying to keep the emotion out of his voice.

Her face brightened like the night sky at sunrise, slowly at first, then blooming fully with a brilliant smile. "Really?"

He steeled himself against the effects of her smile, but had to admit that the sheer joy she seemed to take in caring for the kids won him over and pushed him into the comfort zone of speaking as one caretaker to another. "Sure," he said, then rose from his rocker to take Taylor to her crib. Because it always required two people to put the babies to bed, the kids were accustomed to falling asleep amid hushed conversations. When he settled Taylor in the crib, she twisted the corner of her blanket around her chubby fist but otherwise didn't stir from sleep.

Grant watched Kristen as she took Annie to her crib and settled her in for the night. As Taylor had done, Annie grabbed the satiny rim of her blanket, wrapped it around her fist and continued to sleep. But it was Kristen who held his attention. As if completely enamored with the little girl in the bed, she lingered a few minutes, watching her sleep, fussing with her covers and even bending over the rail of the crib to kiss her smooth forehead before drawing away and turning to leave the nursery.

Grant quietly followed suit, unwittingly enjoying the sensation of sharing the parenting experience with another person, someone who seemed to love the children as much as he did. He didn't want the camaraderie to end, but knew it was inappropriate to go downstairs just for a chat. Then he remembered they'd never discussed the details of her employment. He stifled his instant delight at the thought of spending extra time with her by reprimanding himself for being a poor employer who forgot something so basic.

When she turned to go to her bedroom, he caught her arm. "We never talked about your salary, benefits or even time off," he reminded, smiling slightly. "Maybe we should spend a few minutes in the den now and go over those things?"

Even as he said the last, he realized they were too close. Not only was he holding her satiny arm, but with one slight shift of his other hand he could lift her chin and bring her inviting mouth to within inches of his. He would know if her lips were as soft as they looked and he would know if they tasted as sweet as they seemed.

As if reading his thoughts, Kristen gave him a curious frown and took a step back. "All right," she reluctantly agreed.

She turned to leave ahead of him and Grant whispered a curse. What the hell was happening to him? He knew the facts. He would never get involved with an employee and, like it or not, she worked for him. But even if she didn't work for him, she was too young. She was widowed. And there was too much going on in his life right now to get involved with someone and there was too much confusion in her eyes to let him allow her to get involved with him. As far as he was concerned, they needed to stay away from each other.

But in the den, as he discussed her salary, explained the benefits provided and tried to work out a schedule so that she could have some time off every day, Kristen returned to being her normal friendly self and Grant was overwhelmed by the attraction again. He couldn't help but believe that they were brought together for a reason. Maybe he was being a romantic, but it just seemed incredibly coincidental that a beautiful, friendly, funny, irresistible woman would stumble into his household right at the time that he was looking for someone because he felt alone.

Hell, there was a part of him that actually thought meeting Kristen was his reward for putting up with Mrs. Romani.

Because he had to squelch a laugh at that thought, Grant tried to sober himself and only succeeded in knocking over Chas's pencil holder. Kristen jumped out of her chair.

"Let me get those," she offered.

"No. No," Grant said, waving her back with one hand while he reached for three rolling pencils with the other.

Concerned with grabbing what he could grab before pencils and pens went all over the floor, he didn't realize that their hands were on a collision course for the same pencil. When they brushed—and all they did was brush—Grant felt a jolt of electricity so potent he could have easily fallen back on his chair.

Shocked, he stepped away and let Kristen gather the pencils. Something was here. He *knew* something was here. Something more than he'd ever felt before. Otherwise it wouldn't be so sharp, so immediate, and so very, very powerful.

"There you go," Kristen said, smiling at him as she righted the pencil holder and stood three feet away from him at the side of his desk.

His gaze securely fastened to hers, Grant swallowed, wondering what would happen if he kissed her to test all these feelings he was having. If he kissed her, there was a good possibility he'd discover that these instincts and urges were nothing more than his imagination and he could go back to normal.

Of course, there was also the possibility that she would taste as good as she always smelled, or as sweet as her personality, or as seductively as her looks.

He swallowed again.

"Are you okay?" she asked, peering at him curiously.

He cleared his throat. "I'm fine."

But he wasn't fine. He knew he wasn't fine. He was nuts. Stark-raving mad. Only a lunatic would even consider kissing someone to try to get *rid* of an attraction. Most other men considered kissing women to make them more interested.

He rubbed his hand across the back of his neck. If he didn't put a stop to some of this he would be so far gone he would need therapy.

"Okay. If you're all right, then I'm going to go to my room," Kristen said.

He smiled. "Great."

She began backing out of the den, as if she didn't trust turning her back on him. "Great."

Grant considered being righteously indignant at the way she was carefully edging herself away from him, but he realized that if she knew his thoughts she would probably be running. She slipped from the room and Grant slid into his father's old, worn burgundy leather chair.

If he believed this morning that he was losing it, right now he had to concede that he'd already lost it because he had every intention somehow or another, sometime or another, someway or another of kissing that woman.

He didn't know how, he didn't know when and he wasn't entirely sure why, but at some point nature was going to take over completely and he was going to cover her mouth with his.

And both of them were going to regret it. He'd lose a nanny and she'd lose a job because there was no way they could work together and *live* together with the electricity that simmered between them.

Electricity that would only intensify, he was sure, if he kissed her.

Chapter Four

By the time Kristen had the babies dressed and seated in high chairs waiting to be fed the next morning, she was convinced that Grant Brewster had not been thinking about kissing her the night before. But when he blustered into the kitchen as if nervous and edgy, refused coffee, hardly acknowledged the kids and wouldn't look at her, Kristen started to reconsider. Eventually, though, she persuaded herself to believe that his typically gruff behavior around her was proof that the last thing on his mind would have been wanting to kiss her and she went about her day as if nothing had happened.

Sort of.

Now that she'd opened the floodgates of considering that Grant Brewster might have been tempted to kiss her, she couldn't help but wonder what kissing him would be like. Oh, she had the mechanics of the situation down, it was the emotional end of it that sent a shiver of a thrill through her.

She'd met Bradley Devereaux when she was sixteen and on the backside of her rebellious stage. She supposed she was ready to settle down because the serious young cowboy had calmed her completely. She waited patiently through the two years of friendship it took before he asked her out, and another two years before he asked her to marry him, but she hadn't cared. Bradley Devereaux was the most handsome man she had ever met.

Until Grant Brewster.

Shaking her head, Kristen tried to return her thoughts to spooning lunch into Taylor's mouth, but they refused to budge. She couldn't believe she thought Grant Brewster more handsome than Bradley, but she did. Or maybe she didn't. The difference between Grant and Bradley wasn't so much appearance as disposition. Bradley had been sweet and kind and gentle. Grant could be sweet, kind and gentle with his kids, but with everybody else, he was the seat of command. He relished being in charge.

And that's why she wondered what kissing him would be like. She just wondered if a man of power and influence kissed differently. In fact, if she let her thoughts go too far, she even had to wonder if she could *handle* being kissed by Grant Brewster.

"You throw together one cup of flour, two eggs and some salt. And then beat the daylights out of it," Mrs. Romani said as she snubbed out the cigarette she had been smoking behind the closed door of the laundry room to keep the smoke away from the babies. "Then roll the dough and once it's flat you let it air until it's almost dry. Then you roll it up the same way you would a carpet you need to get off the floor so you can sweep, and you cut the dough into strips no bigger than a quarter-inch." She paused, grimacing. "Got that?"

From the lull in the conversation, Kristen guessed the other party had not "got" it. But when Mrs. Romani hung up the phone with a satisfied smirk, Kristen suspected that might have been deliberate.

"I can't believe these country people think I should just give away my recipes."

"Don't *you?*" Kristen asked incredulously.

"Honey, someday I'm going to write a cookbook and when I do, I'm going to be rich. I'm not giving my recipes away when I could sell them."

Spooning mashed vegetables into Annie's mouth, Kristen said, "I wouldn't consider it giving away your recipes, I'd look at it more like positive PR. If you're smart you could give away just enough of your recipes that you'd whet the appetites of everyone you know. Then when the book came out everybody would want to find out what other great recipes you have and it would be a bestseller."

Mrs. Romani narrowed her eyes. "Crafty one, aren't you?"

"More like practical."

"Then get your head out of the clouds today. Claire is supposed to be here in twenty minutes. You need to get your wits gathered."

Kristen grimaced. "Am I that obvious?"

"Obvious as I was about leaving two ingredients out of that recipe." Mrs. Romani paused in her mission of taking the breakfast dishes out of the dishwasher in anticipation of putting in the lunch load. "So, are you going to tell me what's on your mind?"

Kristen blushed. "It's embarrassingly stupid," Kristen conceded with a laugh.

"What's embarrassingly stupid?" Claire asked, entering the kitchen as she unbuttoned her wool coat.

"Whatever it is that has had Kristen's attention all morning."

"Oh, oh, that can't be good," Claire teased, then immediately reached for Cody who had his arms up and was waiting. She kissed his cheek. "It looks like Mr. Cody wants to play for a few minutes before we put the kids down for a nap. Would you like me to take all three into the family room to play while you eat lunch?"

"I'm not really hungry," Kristen said, eternally grateful Claire changed the subject because, if pressed, she had no idea what she would have said to these people about where her mind had been all morning. After getting up with the babies two nights in a row, she didn't even have the brain-power left to come up with a plausible story to avoid the truth, and she certainly didn't want to tell them she wondered what it would be like to kiss Grant. "But I could use a few minutes upstairs before I tackle another triplet task."

Claire laughed. "I can handle them for an hour of play-time. You go take a nap."

"I don't need a nap," Kristen said, but she involuntarily yawned. "I just need a rest. Maybe I'll read."

"Take a nap," Mrs. Romani said, sidling up behind Kristen. "Chances like this one won't come along often."

Kristen slipped upstairs while Claire and Mrs. Romani carried the kids into the family room. Book in hand, Kristen had every intention of reading for a few minutes to get her perspective back. But reading made her eyelids droop and before she could talk herself out of it, she snuggled into her pillow to take a nap. A while later, she awakened with a start and immediately grabbed her clock, only to discover it was hours later. In fact, it was almost nine o'clock at night.

Nine o'clock!

Grant was going to kill her.

She jumped out of bed and ran downstairs, but all the lights were off. Only the dim glow of a night-light had shown beneath the triplets' nursery, so she knew the babies were in bed, sleeping. Now, she considered that everybody else might be sleeping, too. She combed her fingers through her hair, wondering if she should sneak into Mrs. Romani's room and find out if her destiny had been sealed by her unplanned nap, but when she saw the pale light from the den seeping into the corridor off the foyer she decided to face the music like the mature, intelligent woman she was.

She couldn't hide behind Mrs. Romani's apron forever.

She tiptoed down the hall, accompanied by the light clicking of computer keys. Somewhat surprised that Grant did his own typing, she quietly slipped into the study, trying not to interrupt him. Because he was facing a computer screen, with his back to the door she knew she could wait until it looked as if he was ready for a break or at a good place to stop, and silently slid onto the burgundy leather chair in front of the huge desk.

She watched him type for almost a minute before she started noticing things. First, she realized that his back was broad. The plaid flannel of his shirt stretched across the expanse of his shoulders and tapered down into a trim waist. He had the kind of physique a person couldn't get through anything but hard labor and Kristen guessed that though he was brought up with money and position, Grant was not a man who sat around giving orders. Obviously he'd done his share of the heavy labor. Maybe at the lumber mill. Maybe at his own construction company.

Next she realized that his hair had been cut. He'd left it somewhat shaggy and unruly for his brother's wedding, but now that he'd shaved his beard, it appeared he didn't like the disheveled, disobedient look of the unkempt locks, and the excess hair—the unconventional, disorderly hair—was gone. Making him look as trustworthy and responsible as he truly was.

Finally she noticed that he was a good typist—a fast typist—indicating that he either had plenty of practice or he was working on something that needed to be done as quickly as possible.

As she thought the last, Grant pivoted to get a paper from the desk behind him. Preoccupied, he didn't see her immediately, but caught a glimpse of her in the process of turning to the computer screen again.

He stopped midmotion and Kristen licked her dry lips.

"Hi," she said quietly, trying to sound as innocent as possible given the circumstances.

He faced her, his expression neutral, telling her nothing. "Hi."

"I am really sorry I fell asleep this afternoon."

When she saw that Grant's face was oddly shadowed, Kristen realized that the computer monitor and an old desk lamp were the only sources of light in the room. For all practical intents and purposes they were sitting in the dark. When he peeked across the desk at her, his face shadowed, his eyes shrouded in the kind of concern that gave the room an intimate feeling, Kristen got a quick shiver of regret that she hadn't immediately announced her presence by turning on the overhead light.

As it was, with him gazing at her across the desk and her sitting in virtual darkness, the whole scene was just too familiar and suggestive.

Grant more or less broke the spell by sighing heavily. "No, don't be sorry," he said, but he didn't make any effort to turn on any lights and neither did he make a move to rise and get them out of the circle of privacy they had unwittingly created. "I should have realized that getting up with the triplets two nights in a row would be too much for a rookie."

The reference to sports made her laugh. After years of living with and around men on the ranch it was good to hear a very predictable analogy, one she could relate to.

"I hate to admit this, but it was a little too much to handle because I really am a rookie when it comes to kids."

"And I'm something of a rookie at being the only one in charge of the kids." Getting comfortable, he leaned back on his seat. "I'm not officially complaining, but in my defense I think it's only fair to point out that Chas was supposed to be doing this. While I brought my construction company up from Savannah and started the bidding process on the new mall, he was supposed to handle most of the kid work. His payoff was that he'd use this study as his office and our housekeeper as something of a receptionist."

"How'd Mrs. Romani take that?"

"We didn't have a housekeeper at first, so he didn't have that perk right off the bat, but once we found Mrs. Romani, she loved acting as Chas's receptionist. She loves meeting people at the door, gossiping about their problems and keeping secrets when others were dying to pry them from her meddling lips."

Again, he made her laugh, and though she was enjoying the impromptu camaraderie, and was thoroughly glad she wasn't about to be fired, the air of intimacy settled in more deeply.

She cleared her throat, then asked, "So what happened?"

"Well, Chas fell in love and wanted to get married. Far be it from me to stand in the way of destiny."

Her brows pinched in confusion. "Your brother didn't realize before you guys made your deal that he was getting close enough to a woman that he'd want to marry her?"

"He hadn't met her yet."

"Oh, so you made this deal a while back?"

"No," Grant said in a singsong voice. "We made it about eight weeks ago. And seven weeks ago he met Lily."

"Yikes."

"Yeah, yikes," Grant said, but he laughed, back to being comfortable and relaxed.

Glad to have found a neutral topic to discuss, Kristen said, "So how did he meet her? Was she a client? Did he find her at the lumber mill?"

"Actually," Grant said, stringing out the word until he caught Kristen's gaze. "She was our last nanny."

Their gazes caught and held. Silence fell over them like a cloak. Once again Kristen noticed how dark it was in the room and she realized how easy it would be for two people stuck in the same house, who were sharing the intimate chore of raising children, to become very close. If you added a physical attraction to that closeness...

She leaped from her chair. "You know, I'm still tired. I think I'll just be going back to my room."

As if recognizing his mistake, Grant rose and said, "Don't be silly, you haven't even eaten dinner yet. We saved a little of everything for you. Just come out to the kitchen and I'll heat it up for you."

Oh, no, Kristen thought, but she didn't say it. That would be the last thing she would need. First he was sexy and handsome. Then he won her over with how wonderful he was with the kids. She didn't dare add cooking, which translated to caring for *her,* to that laundry list or she wouldn't stand a chance. Men on a ranch didn't do things like help with dinner—unless they were the cook. Too much exposure to a Renaissance man and she'd be falling at his feet with adoration.

"I'm really not very hungry."

He sighed. "Then cocoa. At least let me make you cocoa."

Since he sounded a little snarly and on the verge of being angry with himself for not noticing that he was pushing her too hard as his nanny, Kristen decided it was safe to accept the simple gesture. The intimacy had vanished from his voice—heck, the courtesy had vanished from his voice. She would be perfectly safe with him. Besides, she really was hungry. Cocoa would at least keep her stomach from growling.

"Okay. That would be great."

Though a low light burned above the butcher block, the very second they entered the kitchen, Grant snapped on the overhead light. Relieved, Kristen walked to one of the tall stools by the white counter. The brightness of the completely white room easily put an end to the intimacy.

"One cup of cocoa, coming right up," Grant said, walking to a cabinet where he extracted a mug.

"Aren't you having any?" Kristen asked, smiling.

He shook his head. "Nope. If anything I might have a cup of coffee. I still have lots of work to do."

"Then it's a good thing I got a long nap," Kristen said, watching him as he retrieved milk from the refrigerator and cocoa from a shelf above the stove. "This way I can get up with the kids again tonight."

He turned and gaped at her. "I thought we already discussed that you've been handling too much of the kid work?"

She shrugged. "Well, yes and no. I mean, getting up two nights in a row when I wasn't used to it was exhausting, but now that I've had a nap I could handle tonight again."

He gave her a long, cool look, his handsome face both accusing and seductive. She seriously wondered if he had any idea how attractive he was, or any idea how his expression made her feel that he could see right into her soul?

"Then what was the deal about needing to go back to bed?"

In that second, from the flicker of emotion in his eyes and the hesitancy in his voice, Kristen knew he understood exactly why she had wanted to escape to her room, but he wasn't deliberately baiting her or taunting her. He was as confused by the potent temptations that continually overwhelmed them as she was and he was either asking for her opinion or seeking permission to discuss the feelings out in the open.

Once again cloaked in an intimacy far too intense for two strangers, she swallowed. She wondered again what kissing him would be like and immediately chastised herself for letting her thoughts go in the very direction they were trying to avoid. First, this man was her boss. Second, she needed to get into his good graces to ask for his assistance in getting her ranch back, and kissing him might temporarily achieve an accord of sorts but could potentially do more harm than good. And, third, her husband might have been gone for over a year, but she'd always believed their love was strong, resilient. A force that couldn't be harmed by time or replaced at whim or will.

She shouldn't be feeling powerful, intimate things for a stranger. It wasn't right.

She cleared her throat. "Look, you're busy and I'm supposed to be the babies' caretaker anyway. I'm just trying to help."

"Then give yourself two minutes of peace and quiet every day."

"I will...when I can." She bit her bottom lip.

Grant cursed, then shoved his fingers through his hair. "I get it. I'm never around so you can't just rest at will."

"I'm not complaining."

That stopped him. Sighing heavily, he turned away from the cocoa he was stirring. "I can see that," he said, then returned his attention to the cocoa again. "I guess Evan and I will have to refine our schedule."

With his neutral tone of voice, Kristen's emotions plummeted to normal again. The temperature of the room went from heated to ordinary so quickly it almost made her dizzy. Still, she certainly wouldn't bring that up for discussion. This subdued, average feeling was exactly what she wanted to feel.

Unfortunately the longer the room remained quiet, the more cozy and familiar it became. Though she warned them not to, her eyes drifted over to the man warming her cocoa and she studied his form, looked at his size, wondered about his textures given that his skin was tanned from outside work and hair-covered. Her thoughts drifted to speculation about why he'd never married, if he'd ever had a long-term serious relationship, then she decided that if he had it would have been in the distant past because he'd gotten wrapped up in caring for the triplets and the economy of this county so effortlessly and so easily that he couldn't have needed to terminate or survive the breakup of a relationship.

But the second those thoughts formed in her brain, she also recognized that he was lonely. Not because she was psychic, but because she could tell from his stance, the rigid way he held his back, the set of his shoulders, that he didn't let anyone share his burdens.

When he turned and caught her staring at him, her face flushed. Shifting her gaze to the countertop, she pretended to dust off a space for him to put her cocoa. Not waiting for her to look up, he slid the cocoa under her nose, as if wanting to make sure she saw it. And when that didn't get her eyes to raise, he hooked his index finger under her chin and lifted her face for her.

"Sometimes when I catch you staring at me I get the feeling you see things no one else sees."

"I'm just a person who knows sadness when they see it," she whispered.

His gaze held hers as he leaned across the counter, getting closer to her. "I'm not sad."

"Lonely, then," she said because she had a compelling urge not to let this go. She knew too much about loneliness to let its mean tentacles ravage another person.

"I didn't even know I was lonely until a couple days ago."

"When your brother got married?"

He licked his lips then, as if involuntarily, his gaze swung down to her mouth and quickly bounced back up again. "Yeah."

Her heart hammered in her chest. The thing that shimmered between them like a living breathing thing was the acknowledgment that she'd entered his life the same day his brother got married. It could have been a coincidence. Or he could be telling her that the strong attraction was the result of emotions created by his brother getting married.

Or he could be telling her that it was easier, less complicated, to blame all this madness on emotions created by his brother's wedding.

She liked that excuse a lot until she remembered that *her* brother had not gotten married. She didn't even have a brother. And she'd gotten accustomed to being alone and lonely a long time ago. She had no excuse for feeling any of the things she felt except that she found the man across the counter attractive.

As if reading her thoughts Grant bent in a little closer. His gaze again dropped to her mouth. For two seconds Kristen contemplated jumping and running, but she couldn't help but recall her thoughts from the afternoon, wondering what it would be like to kiss him. Kissing wasn't a sin or a crime and it didn't necessarily have to lead to anything permanent.

So, she didn't protest when he negated the space between

them. But when his lips lightly brushed hers and she was blasted by a jolt of electricity, she was eternally grateful there was a counter between them. Heat and need seemed to pour from him. Not from loneliness, but from sheer want. He wanted her so much she could feel it. And yearnings double the intensity of anything she'd ever known sprang up within her. One soft touch of his mouth on hers set every inch of her skin to tingling. She'd forgotten that kissing involved so much more than the lips and the quick shiver that danced down her spine almost frightened her. She'd forgotten that when you kissed someone you discovered more than their textures, their scents, their tastes. You learned their feelings, emotions, and even some of their beliefs. And they learned yours. One twenty-second brush of lips left her feeling vulnerable, exposed, and two shakes away from aroused.

Exposed she could handle.

Aroused she could handle.

Vulnerable scared the life out of her.

It didn't take much to pull away. As if testing her commitment to the kiss, Grant didn't have a hold on her. Their only point of contact was their lips. When she broke it, she was free. Except for the fact that their gazes clung and she couldn't seem to tear hers away. Where the kiss had brought her vulnerability, arousal and fear, the expression in his black eyes told her it brought him deeper, darker things. Things that hitched her fear three notches and caused her to jump from her chair.

"I think I better go to my room," she whispered, glad she hadn't said the word bed. She didn't think either one of them could handle it. The very thought almost made her knees buckle, but from the emotion in his eyes, she couldn't quite be sure he wouldn't toss her over his shoulder and take her to one anyway.

"Yeah," Grant said and stepped back.

Kristen watched him lick his lips as if he were determined to remember the taste of her, then she turned and darted out of the kitchen. When she reached the foyer, she started to run and she didn't stop running until her bedroom door was closed behind her.

"What's wrong?"

Though Kristen felt her face heat at Mrs. Romani's gruff question, she managed to smile brightly. "Nothing," she said and put her attention back on the children who were seated around her in a semicircle.

She must have been convincing because Mrs. Romani only said "Hmm" and went back to her crocheting, but when the sound of a car pulling into the driveway invaded the silence, the housekeeper bounced from her seat. "This is where I get lost," she said. "We wouldn't want Grant to find me helping you."

"Actually, Mrs. R," Kristen ventured. "I think he'd be grateful. He told me last night he didn't like the way I kept getting stuck alone with the kids."

Mrs. Romani cackled. "I know he'd be grateful, but he'd also abuse the privilege. There's no way in hell I'm getting dragged too far into this child care. As it is, I'm free to rescue you when you need it. If I actually got involved I'd be nothing but a part of the schedule, and in some respects you'd be alone again."

Though Kristen nodded her understanding, she fervently wished Mrs. Romani didn't feel the need to leave the room. Grant was already gone when Kristen awakened with the triplets, so she hadn't seen him since that kiss and she truly wished their first meeting wouldn't be a private one.

Because she didn't want to talk about it. Not merely because she was flabbergasted by the power of the kiss, but also because she now knew she was a hundred percent right about the differences between Grant and Bradley. The sexual chemistry she felt for Grant was so strong that it was nearly uncontrollable and every time she thought about him she drifted into inappropriate territory. Like making love. She'd known the man four days and already she couldn't stop her daydreams about making love. The worst of it was, she'd let her thoughts go far enough that she actually drew conclusions. Though part of her knew making love with him would be sort of an exhilarating challenge, part was still the young, blushing virgin bride who married her childhood sweetheart. Sex for Kristen had been warm and beautiful. Not edgy. Not compelling. Not overwhelming. But warm. Beautiful.

Grant picked that exact second to walk into the family room and though Kristen tried to avoid it, their gazes collided. Again her thoughts jumped to her analysis of what making love should be and trapped in the gaze of the tall, dark, handsome man in the doorway the last word her mind reached for was beautiful. She thought powerful. She suspected greedy. She had thoughts of yearning and need. But there was no way her mind would shift to warm or beautiful.

In the very second that she decided she had to stay away from him—whatever the cost—Claire slipped into the room from behind him. "Hello, everybody," she sang, sliding out of her winter coat.

Kristen wondered if it was an accident that Claire had arrived the same time as Grant, or if he planned it because he couldn't stop thinking about her the way she couldn't stop thinking about him, and he had also drawn the same conclusions she had. They shouldn't have a relationship—couldn't, actually. They were two completely different people, opposites. If that kiss last night taught them nothing else, Kristen had to concede it proved they were far too different to ever get along in the way their bodies seemed to want to get along.

"Hi, Claire," Kristen said, pulling her gaze away from Grant Brewster's dark, hypnotizing eyes. "How was your day at work?"

"She was a monster on the phone with suppliers," Evan said, as he, too, entered the family room. Shrugging out of his overcoat, he laughed with glee. "Then she tried to tell me that being willful and demanding was something my father taught her."

"He did!" Claire protested indignantly.

"I'll bet," Evan joked, lowering himself to the floor with the triplets, good suit and all.

In that second, Kristen decided that even if Grant hadn't organized this little family reunion, it was a welcome buffer. The presence of two other people took the tone of the room from heated and edgy to cool and composed without so much as a ripple of difficulty. "You two wouldn't by any chance be staying for supper?"

"If Mrs. Romani's making spaghetti," Evan said. "*I* could be persuaded."

"And I can be persuaded anytime I don't have to cook," Claire chimed in. "Besides, I'm starting to feel a little guilty about leaving you alone with the kids so much. So how about if we stay for dinner, then Evan and I will play with the kids and even get them ready for bed?"

"Sounds great to me," Kristen said. She loved these babies with her whole heart and soul, but she had no idea caring for babies could be so—constant. If it weren't for Mrs. Romani, she wouldn't even get to go to the bathroom.

"Good," Evan said, rising from the floor. "I'll just go sweet-talk Mrs. Romani into putting more spaghetti in the pot."

"And I'll help," Claire said, also pushing herself off the floor.

"And I think I'll take advantage of this minute to go upstairs and change. For once I'd like to eat dinner in something that isn't speckled with baby food."

They left the room quickly and casually, as if nothing was amiss, but Kristen didn't dodge the look Grant gave her as she happily left him with the babies.

He *wanted* to be alone with her. She could see it in his eyes. But at this point she was terrified to be alone with him. Not because she was afraid of him, but because she was afraid of her own reactions to him.

Chapter Five

When Kristen heard one of the babies crying, she bounced up in bed, glanced at the clock and saw it was morning and time to get up anyway.

After a satisfied stretch, she slipped into her robe and slippers and padded across the hall. Things couldn't have gone better the night before if she'd planned them. As if everything were perfectly normal, Grant ate dinner with them, but excused himself shortly thereafter to do some work in the den. As had been arranged, Kristen went directly to her room, leaving Evan and Claire to care for the babies. She took a leisurely shower, read for several hours and drifted off into a comfortable sleep for the first time in days.

Now it was morning. Six o'clock. And for the past two days Grant had been gone by six o'clock. So she had nothing to worry about and at least ten full hours of uninterrupted time with the kids. She was getting very good at taking care of them. Both girls and even Cody were content with her. The Brewsters were learning to trust her.

Things could not be any better.

Happy, smiling, she opened the nursery door only to find Grant waiting for her. Seated on one of the three rockers, he held Annie who was guzzling milk as if she hadn't been fed in days.

"Good morning."

Kristen cleared the sleep from her throat. "Good morning."

"Before we go any further, I want to apologize for my behavior two nights ago," Grant said, his voice tight with controlled anger. "I had every intention of apologizing when I arrived home yesterday and I almost resent the fact that you invited Claire and Evan to stay for dinner as if you were afraid I was going to attack you. You don't need chaperons. You're perfectly safe with me."

Kristen gasped. "I didn't invite them because I was afraid you were going to attack me!"

Still angry, he caught her gaze. "You certainly behaved like it."

"Well, I didn't mean to," Kristen insisted, embarrassed.

With that out in the open, the nursery got incredibly quiet. If there had been a clock in the room, Kristen was sure she could have heard its ticking.

Sighing heavily, Grant lifted Annie to his shoulder to burp her. "At the risk of sounding redundant and stupid," he said, more nicely this time, "I'm going to apologize again."

Knowing she had to accept this gracefully, Kristen nodded.

"But I'm not going to try to pretend I don't find you attractive," Grant continued, causing heat to suffuse Kristen's cheeks again. "Because I think you're *very* attractive," he admitted. "But you're perfectly safe with me. I need you more as a nanny than a lover."

Though he'd intended them to be reassuring, his words

spiraled through her and for a fleeting second, Kristen wished, again, that she could be his lover. Even if it was only once, if only to have a taste of how wonderful, how passionate, it would be to make love to a man like Grant.

But instead of voicing that unwelcome confession, Kristen said, "I accept your apology..." Her chin lifted. "And for the record I'm *not* afraid of you."

Because she worked so hard to keep her voice level and her emotions at bay, her words came out harsh, almost prudish. When Grant set his jawline, she wondered if she had insulted him again, but decided she couldn't care. It was better to have him on her side as a nanny, than a lover, and this conversation had accomplished that perfectly. All she had to do was get out without pulling them into their attraction again.

Backing to the door, she said, "Since you seem to have everything under control in here, I'm going to get my shower."

She didn't give him a chance to respond, but once the door had closed behind her, Grant cursed a blue streak. *She was afraid of him.* All this time he'd thought her responses to him proved she was attracted to him, when the truth appeared to be that she actually feared him. He almost couldn't believe it. Never in his entire life had a woman been afraid of him.

He'd had women want him. He'd even had women *hate* him. But he'd never had one terrified of him. He had never had to deal with a woman who jerked every time he touched her and ran from the room every time they were alone and he wasn't quite sure what, if anything, he should do about it.

In some respects it made fighting his attraction to her easy. As long as she continued to look at him with fear in her eyes, he'd certainly stay the hell away from her. But, she was also his nanny. Living in his house. He couldn't allow a person who lived in his house to fear him. That wouldn't be fair. She'd be uncomfortable and restless all the time and eventually the pressure would get to her and she'd leave. And he couldn't afford for her to leave. Nannies didn't grow on the trees in Brewster County, Pennsylvania, and for three men trying to raise sibling triplets a nanny was essential.

He had no choice but to make her comfortable, not just with the kids, but also with him. And that meant he had to get her to like him.

Like him.

Not love him. Not sleep with him—though the thought was immensely tempting—just *like him.* Surely he could handle that.

The first step to getting Kristen to like him, Grant decided, was to spend more time at home. Part of her fear of him might stem from dislike, and her dislike could stem from the way that he overworked her.

Which meant he couldn't overwork her anymore.

"I can't have a conference call tonight," he said into the receiver of the phone on his father's desk. Phase one had been to move most of his work into the home office, at least until Chas returned. Phase two was to restructure his work hours and work schedule.

"Look, Hunter, I know that the faster we get everything organized, the faster we can move into the next project, but my brother just got married last weekend. I have triplets to look after."

Sighing as he listened to his partner comment on that, Grant rubbed his fingers over his eyes. "Yes, we hired a nanny, but I can't completely leave the care of three babies to one person. You know things would go a lot smoother on this project, if you'd just come home.''

Because Hunter couldn't find an answer for that because he didn't want to come home, they finished the remainder of their business and set the conference call for ten o'clock the next morning, suiting Grant's schedule perfectly. Pleased, and ready to put into motion phase three of his plan, Grant rose from his seat and strode into the corridor and through the foyer. If his guess was correct, this was prebed snack time for the triplets and like a good guardian, Grant decided he would be part of it.

''Hey, guys,'' he said and he strode through the swinging door to the kitchen. Looking like two little angels, Annie and Taylor grinned up at him. It appeared more cookie had gone around their mouths than into their stomachs, but that only made him smile. ''I see it's cookie time for the Brewster girls.''

Annie screeched with joy. Taylor pounded the flat of her chubby little hand on the tray of her high chair.

''Actually they're having crackers tonight.''

That made Grant frown. ''Why not cookies? They like cookies better.''

''Cookies are full of sugar,'' Kristen pointed out. ''Look at them. Annie has enough energy to run the Boston Marathon. Taylor could fight Joe Louis. The last thing they need is more sugar.''

Proud of her for coming up with that assumption, Grant caught Kristen's gaze and smiled his approval. When her response was to back away from him, Grant realized she probably didn't understand that the smile was confirmation that he believed she was doing well. So, he came right out and said it. ''Good work,'' he praised, pulling out a chair so he could sit in front of the girls' high chairs. ''Good thinking. I'm proud of you.''

"Thanks," Kristen said, but Grant noted that she continued to hang back, away from the girls...away from him. "I can handle the girls myself," she said. "So you can return to the study and finish your work."

"My work is finished. At least, as much I can do for one night. Besides, I want to spend some time with the girls."

"Oh," Kristen said, sounding flustered. "Do you want me to leave?"

His forehead furrowed. "No. I thought we'd take care of bath time together."

"But one person can handle bath time alone..."

If it hadn't been his mission to get Kristen to like and trust him, Grant would have offered to give her the night off.

"I know it only takes one person, but it will be easier with two."

"It just seems that two people handling the job of one person is a waste of energy."

He frowned at her. "Are you tired, Ms. Devereaux?"

She shook her head. "No."

"Is there something you want to do right now, other than bathe the kids?"

"No."

He smiled pleasantly. "Then let's just take the kids upstairs, give them a leisurely bath, feed them a bottle and put them to sleep. Then we can both have the rest of the night off."

Returning his smile the best she could, Kristen nodded. But she couldn't stop thinking about the fact that he'd kissed her. Not the action itself, not even really the repercussions or ramifications of being kissed by a boss. No, if her thoughts had been as simple and uncomplicated as that she could have handled them. In fact, it wasn't actually thoughts that bothered her, but feelings. Looking at him, she could feel the press of his mouth on hers and once her brain took her to that point everything else was a matter of chain reaction. Her blood heated. Her heart seemed to freeze. Tingles raced down her spine.

She reminded herself of a woman who had just received her first kiss and kept reliving it for the sheer joy of remembering every delicious second of the passion. But since she'd been kissed before, many times, particularly by a man she adored, it confused her that one damned peck on the lips could nearly paralyze her.

"Come on, Taylor," Grant said, pulling her from her high chair and lifting her over his head.

"You're going to get cracker in your hair," Kristen cautioned, but more as self-defense than anything else. For some reason or another the nicer he was with the children, the more she remembered him kissing her. And the tension. She could feel the unbearable tension any time he got within five feet of her, as if something was missing.

Did she *want* him to kiss her again?

No. That was stupid. And wrong. Basically she was here under false pretenses and until she confessed who she was and what she wanted she couldn't share anything as intimate as a kiss. She had to keep this relationship completely platonic.

She slid Annie out of her high chair and was rewarded by a quick, cracker covered kiss and stopped dead in her tracks. Though she'd kissed the kids a hundred time, nuzzled them and offered affection in many different forms, it was the first time any of the kids had spontaneously given affection to her.

"Oh, Annie," she said and nestled her nose against the baby's soft, light brown hair. "That was so sweet."

"Now, look who's getting cracker on her face," Grant said, and as automatically as Annie had kissed her, he turned and brushed his thumb across her lips, wiping away the crumbs and setting off a band of awareness rippling through Kristen.

Without regard for the consequences, she looked up at him and found him staring down at her. Each of them held a chubby, squirming ten-month-old baby girl, but neither of them seemed to notice that. Every time he touched her, something happened between them. Something physical. Something very real.

She took a step back, breaking the contact, and pivoted toward the kitchen door. "Come on, Annie," she said, ignoring the tingling awareness, forgetting the electricity that had just zapped her, and fully intending to have her head examined when she returned to Texas. "Let's get you ready for bed."

Grant followed her, but Kristen paid no attention to him. She paid little attention to him the entire time they bathed the children, fed them a bottle and rocked them to sleep. She leaned on the excuse that they needed to be quiet for the babies to settle down and drift off to dreamland, but the truth was Grant Brewster had her officially confused. She had met and married the love of her life years ago. She *wasn't* wrong. And that meant she *couldn't* be attracted to Grant Brewster. It cheapened everything she felt for Bradley. And she absolutely refused to let it happen.

Grant concluded it was time to try another tack. If he couldn't even brush a few crumbs off her face without her jumping with fear, then things were a lot worse than he'd thought. That being the case, he decided to shift gears. If it killed him, this woman would like and trust him by the end of the week.

"I thought you might like a night out," he said from behind the cover of the newspaper the next morning.

"What's a night out?" Mrs. Romani said, then, again, laughed at her own joke.

"You get plenty of time off," Grant reminded her, peeking at the pushy old woman who wouldn't even do the babies' laundry until they raised her salary.

Smiling pleasantly, she shrugged and went back to flipping pancakes.

"What do you think, Kristen?" he asked, directing his attention to her.

Kristen only stared at him. "What would I do?"

"Well, why not call Claire and see if she wants to go to a movie or something?"

"I thought you'd be asking her to help with the kids."

"Evan and I will take care of the kids," he said immediately, blocking her argument because he knew that once she had a night off, a night away, she'd stop thinking of him as a slave driver.

"I guess it would be okay."

"I think it's a great idea," Mrs. Romani piped in from the stove. "I hear Evan's car coming up the driveway. You can make arrangements now and that way things will be all set for tonight."

Nodding carefully, Kristen seemed to agree. She even seemed to be happy about the deal as she made plans with Claire, but Grant got an odd sense, again, that something wasn't right here. If she only needed time away from the kids, she wouldn't look so confused.

Which almost made him curse. Now, not only was she afraid of him, but it appeared she might be considering leaving if he didn't do something drastic.

"I don't really feel much like a movie," Claire said as she maneuvered her husband's sports utility vehicle on the town's main street. "But what I do feel like is a great big piece of chocolate pie and a scoop of vanilla ice cream."

Kristen couldn't stop her mouth from watering. "That does sound good."

"Great," Claire said, then quickly slipped the fancy truck into a parking place in front of the diner. She nodded in the direction of the blinking neon sign that said only Diner. "It doesn't look like much, but the pies here are heavenly."

Not needing to be persuaded, Kristen jumped out and waited for Claire to meet her by the door before she walked inside.

The place was small, overlit and squeaky-clean. Following Claire's lead, Kristen took a seat on one of the red plastic stools by the shiny red counter. Immediately, a tall redhead walked over. The pin on the white lapel of her pink waitress uniform gave her name as Abby.

"What can I do for you tonight, ladies?" she asked pleasantly.

"We're having pie, Abby," Claire said, then faced Kristen. "Kristen, this is my best friend in the world, Abby Conway."

Abby grinned at her. "Pleased to meet you."

"It's nice to meet you, too," Kristen said, but she felt uncomfortable. She should have recognized that Claire would have friends—probably tons of friends given her congenial nature—and wondered why she had thought this would be a quiet, peaceful night out.

"Coffee with that pie?" Abby asked.

"Only if it's decaf," Claire said. "Or I'll never get to sleep tonight."

"Me, too," Kristen seconded. "I never know what time the girls will get up, so I like to get most of my sleep before three."

As Abby reached into the pie shelf to get the thick chocolate pie, Claire said, "Kristen is watching the triplets. She really hasn't had much of a day off since Chas is out of town, but once he gets back she'll be okay."

"What's the matter? Grant too good to help with the girls?"

"Grant's really busy," Kristen answered without thinking and the little section of the diner in which she sat suddenly got incredibly quiet.

As if in slow motion, both Claire and Abby turned to look at her.

"Really?" Abby said, her brows arching.

Appalled at her lack of discretion, Kristen turned to Claire. "I'm sorry, am I not supposed to talk about the big project he's working on?"

Claire laughed and batted a hand in dismissal. "Abby and I couldn't care less about Grant's projects." She braced her elbow on the counter and rested her head on her closed fist as if preparing to listen closely. "We do, however, find it interesting that you were so quick to defend him. What gives?"

Abby set the pie in front of Kristen and Claire.

"Nothing," Kristen said, but she knew her face flamed with color.

"Oh, Lord, it's the Brewster nanny curse striking again," Abby said, then she laughed heartily. "This is great!"

"What's great?" Kristen asked.

Claire patted her hand. "Abby gets bored here at the diner and makes more of things than they need to be. In this case, she's talking about the fact that I volunteered to help the Brewsters with the babies first and I ended up married to Evan. Then Chas hired Lily, and Lily swept him off his feet. Now, here you are, working to help the Brewsters with their babies and you seem a little quick to defend the only Brewster that's still a bachelor."

Kristen's eyes bulged. "You think I'm going to marry him?"

Abby leaned in and whispered to Kristen. "That's the curse."

Kristen looked from Abby to Claire. "You call it a curse to be married to a Brewster?"

Claire laughed. "No, marrying a Brewster is great. They're strong, loyal, sexy..." She caught Kristen's gaze. "Incredibly sexy men who treat their wives as partners. I don't think it's a curse. I think we should start calling it the Brewster Blessing."

Abby only said, "Humph," and walked away, but Claire laughed again.

"She's known the Brewsters forever and loves them like brothers," Claire said, then she giggled with glee. "Hey, maybe that's why she calls it a curse."

"Maybe," Kristen said, filling her mouth with pie so she couldn't say any more. For her, it was a curse to be so blasted attracted to one of the men who had custody of her triplets. Not only was she weaving silly fantasies, but she was getting soft, starting to think that asking them to give up custody was wrong, because they loved these children so much. Talking with Claire and Abby, hearing the respect and love for the Brewsters in their voices, didn't help Kristen much.

In fact, it made her feel guilty, until she awakened the next morning and found herself sitting across the breakfast table from Grant Brewster again. Dressed in a work shirt and jeans, with his hair neatly combed and busy reading the paper, he looked like a strong, capable, loving family man—exactly as Claire had said. Since he'd not only helped her dress the girls, but feed them breakfast, he'd chipped another wedge into her heart and that just couldn't do. She wasn't here to fall in love—or even in lust—or even into a flirtatious attraction. She had real, serious business with this man, and she wouldn't be able to accomplish any of her purposes unless he saw her as a mature, intelligent woman. And he wouldn't see her as a mature, intelligent woman if she kept giving him puppy-dog eyes, mooning over him every time he cuddled a child.

"Don't you have work to do?" she asked more curtly than she intended. Abby was right. She was cursed.

"I'm working in the den today," Grant said, then turned the page of the newspaper. "Why? Is there something you'd like to do today?"

"No," she said, then swore in her head. He had to stop being nice to her. The nicer he was the more she liked him. Actually the more time he spent around the house, the more she liked him. Which was worse! And which meant she had to get out of the kitchen.

"I'm going to shower and dress, then I'll handle playtime this morning."

Grant put down the paper. "What kinds of games are they playing now?"

"Peekaboo. Toss the ball. Patty-cake. Animal sounds... the usual," Kristen said, though she had no idea if that was usual or not.

"Anybody say a real word yet?"

"Boo and who and do," Kristen said, then she laughed because even though they were real words, they were also nothing more than sounds. "Why? Are you waiting for something specific?"

"No, I'm just curious. You know what?" he said, and rose from his seat. "While you're taking your shower, I'm going to check the Internet and see if I can find a Web site on child development," he said, then pulled Annie out of her high chair. He nuzzled his nose against her neck. "I'd

like to see if the kids are where they're supposed to be, and
see if there are things we should be working to teach them.''

"That's so sweet," Kristen said before she could stop
herself. "I mean, it's a sweet idea to find a good way to
use playtime," she said, improvising an excuse even though
it didn't make a great deal of sense. Knowing she had to
get herself the heck out of the room, she started backing
toward the door. "I'll be down in about twenty minutes."

Grant smiled at her. "The kids and I will be in the den."

But the second she was out of the kitchen, Grant's smile
faded. She was even more nervous around him now than
she was yesterday. It seemed that everything he did to make
her see his interest was in the kids, caring for the kids, and
being a decent person in general, only seemed to make her
all the more wary.

"Unless Claire and Abby said something to her last
night," he said, not realizing his thoughts were out loud.

"I have no idea," Mrs. Romani said, reaching for her
ever-present pack of cigarettes. "But I do know it's time
for a break," she added and started walking toward the back
door.

"You should quit those things," Grant called after her,
truly concerned for her health, then he shook his head in
wonder. Now he was even starting to be nice to their housekeeper! The woman who monitored his pancake intake as
if he were fat. The woman who refused to care for his
babies!

That was it. The end. Tonight he was going to get Kristen
Devereaux to like him. So he could stop all this madness.
If he had to stand on his head and whistle "Dixie," the
woman was going to admit to him that he was a good, kind,
decent person and she wasn't afraid of him.

Chapter Six

"**Y**ou want me to what?"

Grant peered at his grumpy housekeeper through narrowed eyes. He wasn't sure how it had happened but he liked her. Somehow over the course of the past week, she'd edged her way around his defenses and he cared enough that he wished she would quit smoking. Since that miracle had occurred, since a woman who fought him tooth and nail could work her way into his good graces, Grant decided a man as truly decent and kind as he was should be able to talk Kristen Devereaux into liking him.

"Just watch the babies long enough for Kristen and me to have a private dinner."

Her eyebrows rose.

"It's not what you're thinking," he protested, immediately guessing her assumption.

"Pity," she said, walking away from him to stir a pot of something boiling on the stove. "It would certainly solve a lot of problems if you and Kristen did hook up romantically."

He scowled at her. He did not think it would solve a lot of problems. He knew it would create problems. For Pete's sake the woman was his employee.

"So will you do it?"

"I'd be more tempted if you told me this was a seduction dinner."

"And I'd be more tempted to give you regular raises if you could once in your life cooperate."

Tilting her head, she considered that. "Sounds reasonable," she said, then she smiled.

That flabbergasted him. "It does?"

She shrugged. "Sure."

Grant didn't know what kind of magic was happening here, but he got the sudden and distinct impression that Kristen had something to do with it.

While she was upstairs playing with the triplets, Grant set the table. He put out the good dishes. He dug out the crystal. He even used the family silver. Eyeing the table critically, he recognized that it was in desperate need of something pretty in the middle but, as a man, he didn't have a clue what to use. Without so much as a second thought, he slid the cell phone from his pocket and dialed the number of the florist, explaining that he wanted something nice for the table for dinner.

Within minutes, he had flowers.

The centerpiece of red, yellow and pink roses accented by white mums was bright and cheerful without being overstated. It was exactly what he needed.

Because the dining room was off by itself and not a room used as a through way for traffic, it was easy to keep Kristen out while they fed the children and while he took a shower and changed clothes. It wasn't precisely his intention to look nice "for" her, but he did want to look nice "to" her. Just a nuance of difference, but Grant was beginning to see it made all the difference in the world. He finally recognized that as long as he continued to wear the rugged, outdoor clothes of a man who spent most of his day doing heavy labor, he would continue to give her the feeling that he was somehow stronger, more powerful than she was and that wasn't true. As far as he was concerned all people were created equal.

When he reentered the kitchen, he found Kristen curiously lifting the lids off the pots on the stove only to find each one empty.

"I asked Mrs. Romani to put our dinner in serving dishes and set it on the dining-room table."

At the sound of his voice she turned and he watched her gaze slither from the top of his head to the tips of his toes. Good, he thought, standing still for her scrutiny. In Dockers and a sport shirt he knew he looked absolutely tame. Nice, even. Definitely friendly.

When she brought her confused gaze to his face, he smiled.

Kristen swallowed.

"Why are we eating in the dining room?"

"Because it doesn't hurt for us to behave like adults every once in a while," he said, then extended his arm, indicating that she should leave the kitchen with him. "It might be true that we have three kids, but that doesn't mean our whole lives should revolve around them. Now and again, we should take a minute to pamper ourselves."

In a way, Kristen agreed with him. Sort of. At least she understood what he meant. She'd grown so accustomed to sitting on the floor and talking in short sentences with even shorter words while using a singsong voice, that she felt as if she could have her own segment of "Sesame Street," maybe even her own show on public television.

What troubled her was that they were doing this mature,

adult dinner alone. She glanced at his clothes, then her own. And he'd dressed for this. She still wore jeans and a sweater.

When he opened the door and the scent of roses hit her, Kristen licked her dry lips. Roses, at least three dozen accented by white mums, decorated an already stunning table. For a man who said he was attracted to her, but not going to do anything about it, Grant was sending some very mixed signals.

Nonetheless, she decided she'd take him at his word and assume his actions were as innocent as he seemed to intend.

"Here, let me get that," he said when Kristen reached to pull out her own chair at the table. Warm, spicy aromas of something Italian drifted to her and Kristen stifled the urge to inhale deeply.

"This looks and smells wonderful," Kristen said as Grant walked up behind her and slid her chair from beneath the table.

"Yes, it does," he agreed, but because he was directly behind her, bending slightly to position her chair as she sat, his innocent words whispered across her neck in a most seductive fashion and Kristen had to fight a shiver. When the scent of aftershave glided around from behind her, Kristen's eyes widened involuntarily, and every nerve ending of her body went on red alert. But superseding that, Kristen got the delightful feeling that she was a princess. She'd never seen a table this beautiful with an antique lace tablecloth, real crystal, shiny silver.

"I asked Mrs. Romani to make manicotti for us tonight. I hope you don't mind," Grant said, as he handed her a small pitcher, which contained salad dressing.

"No, I love manicotti," Kristen said, taking the container from his hand and using the petite ladle to cover her lettuce, tomatoes and cucumbers with the golden dressing.

Grant smiled at her. "Great because it's my favorite."

Kristen was about to tell him that manicotti was her favorite Italian dish, too, as she felt the click of rightness between them again. But she remembered what Abby and Claire had told her about the Brewster curse, and reminded herself that such close quarters did strange things to people. She didn't want to make too much out of every little thing, not merely because she didn't want to make a fool of herself, but also because she wasn't really here as a nanny. She was Taylor, Cody and Annie's aunt, here to try for custody. When Grant found that out, she wanted him to be glad he met her, glad he knew her, comfortable with the fact that she was another relative for the children, not furious because she deceived him.

She cleared her throat, then realized that in seeking to sound casual, she'd just made herself sound nervous.

"Roll?"

Kristen accepted the basket Grant handed to her. Striving for nonchalance, she attempted a smile for him, but when she actually looked at him, their gazes caught and held and Kristen couldn't even breathe.

His eyes weren't amber or cinnamon, they were a deep, dark brown, surrounded by thick lashes that made them appear even darker. But there was a softness in their expression that didn't hint at vulnerability, but more at kindness or goodness. He certainly wasn't gentle or soft, but he was good and he was kind.

And everything about him drew her.

"Yes, I'd love a roll, thank you," Kristen said, yanking the basket from his hands and her attention away from places it shouldn't go. She didn't know why she could see the things in him that other people seemed to miss. She didn't know why he let her see them. All she knew was that she couldn't get too personal, too private with this man unless she wanted to admit who she was. Since she couldn't yet do that, she had to keep this dinner as platonic as possible.

"So, are you a football fan?"

He looked at her. "Excuse me?"

"Football," she repeated. "Do you like football?"

"Yes and no," Grant said. "If Penn State is doing well everyone within a three-hundred-mile radius is a fan. On their off years, we can ignore them with a clear conscience."

"Fair-weather fan?"

His forehead furrowed. "It's a little hard to get interested in someone who is losing. What about you? Are you a football fan?"

"It's a law in Texas that you have to cheer for the Cowboys, but as for actually watching the games, I fall short."

The conversation died a quick, natural death and the only sound in the room quickly became the clicking of silverware. Kristen racked her brain for something to talk about other than the children but everything that came to mind was too personal. She was curious about why he'd never married. She wanted to know if he'd ever had a serious relationship. She wanted to know why he felt so responsible for grown brothers. But more than any of those, she wanted to know, really wanted to know, if he was feeling any better about the loss of his father. Not only because she felt guilty since she knew she held a piece of the puzzle that might help him understand, but also because she'd been through grief. She knew how important it was to have someone to talk to.

"So what about—"

"How are you—"

Because they'd started their questions at exactly the same time, both backed off, smiling.

Grant said, "You first."

"No, maybe you'd better go. I think my question might have been inappropriate."

"Oh, now you have me curious," he said, pushing aside his salad dish and offering her the manicotti.

"Well," she said, busying herself with serving the main course. She couldn't ask about his grief. If she talked about his father and her sister without revealing who she was, it would be too misleading. But since her comment demanded that she ask something personal, she said, "It's none of my business so if you don't want to answer you don't have to, but I was wondering why you haven't married."

Grant also occupied himself with the manicotti as he spoke. "I've never actually thought about it," he admitted and Kristen could tell it was an honest answer.

"Not at all?"

"Never," he said, still occupying himself with getting food.

"Right woman never came along?"

He took his time about responding and for a few seconds, Kristen felt he wouldn't. But suddenly, unexpectedly, he glanced at her. "I guess marriage didn't enter my mind because no woman ever made me *want* to be married."

His very informative answer caused Kristen to thank her lucky stars that she had practical, relevant reasons not to fall for this man who would only hurt her if she did. Presumably out of self-defense, Grant changed the subject and came up with several neutral topics they could discuss through dinner. Before she realized it was happening, he actually had her laughing. But when the hour had passed in a blur of laughter and casual friendship, Kristen felt the nudge again, the sharp snap of recognition that there was something special in the air. For two people who didn't seem to have anything in common, they could certainly find enough things to talk about. And they could make each other laugh. And they were incredibly comfortable.

Which made her incredibly uncomfortable. She wanted him to like and trust her. And she was accomplishing that. But she hadn't expected to like and trust him in the bargain. At least not this much, *or in this way.*

"Mrs. Romani made cake for dessert," Grant said.

"Oh, no," Kirsten said with a groan. "I couldn't possibly eat another bite."

"Coffee, then?"

She shook her head. "I won't be able to sleep if I drink coffee," she said, but in truth, she knew she had to get away from him. Peeking at the gorgeous floral arrangement and the good dishes and silver, and having experienced the wonderful camaraderie over dinner, she suddenly wondered if he hadn't done all this for the purpose that almost seemed obvious. He didn't need to make her his friend. He didn't need to make her like and trust him. He already had custody of the kids. He didn't need to get her permission to take them or to prove that he'd be a good caretaker if he did.

So why the heck had he gone to all this trouble?

With her mind not occupied with conversation, but on the dynamics of what was going on around her, Kirsten felt a shiver of fear. Real fear. Not because she was afraid of Grant, but because she was afraid of herself. She reacted to Grant in ways that were completely inappropriate. Romantic ways that filled her head with unsuitable notions. She could ruin this whole deal if she let her instincts take her somewhere she didn't want to go, and right now her intuition was very strong and very clear. She genuinely liked this man and she had a sneaking suspicion he liked her, too.

If the flowers, dishes and crystal were anything to go by, he also had no trouble admitting it. If the scene itself was anything to go by, she would think he was trying to seduce her...

Which was absurd. Ludicrous.

He smiled at her and set his hand on the table only inches from hers and Kristen swallowed.

Or was it ludicrous? The truth could be that she'd unwittingly fallen into a trap, created by a master seducer. He'd said he'd never thought of marriage, yet a man like him couldn't have—wouldn't have—been celibate all his life. Which meant he not only could be seducing her, but he could be doing it with no thought for tomorrow. And it would be the kids who would suffer if she didn't—or couldn't—resist him.

"Well, let's get these dishes to the kitchen," she said enthusiastically and bounced from her seat because the cure for this wonderful friendly dinner, which could tumble into romantic with the slightest push, was to make sure that no one had the opportunity to push it.

He waved her back down. "Mrs. Romani's agreed to clean up in the morning. Just sit. Relax a minute."

"I don't like leaving dishes for someone else."

Grant snickered. "Trust me. She's paid very well to do them."

"Well, I feel awkward. Uncomfortable," she said and Grant studied her.

For the entire hour they ate, she was perfectly comfortable. Friendly even. Now that she recognized she'd been lulled into liking him, it seemed she was trying to change her own mind. Well, he'd be darned if he'd let her. He hadn't gone through all this just to have her erase all his good deeds like notes from a chalkboard. Bonds had been formed tonight. Bridges were built. He would not let her avoid or ignore them.

"There's no need to feel awkward or uncomfortable,

Kristen,'' he said softly. ''Though I think I understand why you're a little nervous, I want to tell you that there's no reason to be. You can trust me.''

''I can?'' Kristen said and immediately shifted away from him, stiffening with fear.

He almost cursed. ''Why do you feel you can't? I've never given you any reason in the world to dislike me and we both know that the truth is we want this.''

''I don't think so,'' Kristen said, inching away from him again.

''Why not?'' Grant said as he rose and walked over to pull out her chair. ''We're both adults, Kristen. There's no reason to feel ill at ease about this.''

He was so close Kristen could smell his cologne and for two seconds she actually contemplated letting him seduce her. Because he was right. She did want this. She wanted it so much it shamed her.

Purely for self-defense, she grabbed her dish and silver. ''Let me clear the table.''

He sighed. ''I'll help.''

''No. No,'' Kristen insisted. ''You go on.''

''No,'' Grant said, equally stubborn. ''I'm not letting you get out of this so easily.''

Kristen's cheeks burned. ''Boy, you certainly take the cake. You're so sure of yourself.''

He glared at her. ''Why shouldn't I be?''

''Are you that conceited that you think every woman in the world wants to be seduced by you?''

''Seduced by me?'' Grant sputtered. He stared at her for a few seconds then burst out laughing. ''Honey, I wasn't trying to seduce you, I was trying to get you to like me. For the past few days I've felt you were walking on eggshells around me and I was trying to make you more at ease.''

As Kristen felt the flames of embarrassment lick every inch of her body, Grant enjoyed a good belly laugh.

"Well, thank you very much for making me feel stupid," she said and grabbed another dish from the table to throw it on her growing stack. With no regard for chipping good china or ruining good crystal, she tossed and shoved the utensils into a large pile.

"Oh, I'm sorry, Kristen," he said, as he obviously tried to subdue his chuckles. "But you have to admit it is funny."

"I don't see anything funny about it at all," she said, fuming that he apparently considered her so far out of his league that he couldn't stop laughing. "I'm not completely unattractive or without my own personal charms. If I wanted to seduce you I probably would have been more successful than you were at seducing me."

He turned serious so quickly, Kristen didn't see it coming.

"But I hadn't tried to seduce you," he said softly. "If I'd tried, I would have succeeded."

"Huh!" she said, then slammed a spoon on a dish. "Fat chance."

"Oh, really," he said, grabbing her wrist to stop her cleanup efforts, then gently sliding his fingers under the rim of her sweater sleeve.

Tingles of awareness danced up her arm but, stubborn, insulted, she ignored them and spun away.

He pulled her around to face him again. "You started this," he reminded quietly. "You questioned my sex appeal and my abilities. I can't let this go unchallenged."

"You could try," Kristen said breathlessly, but deep down inside she desperately hoped he wouldn't. Every inch of her skin was on fire and her lips longed to kiss him again. The consequences of these wants and yearnings drifted out of her mind. With them, they took the repercussions and ramifications. All she could see and think about were his compelling black eyes, and the fact that she seemed to be able to see right into his soul when she looked into them.

"I don't really think you want me to," he said, then breached the short distance between them and pressed his mouth to hers.

The kiss was unlike anything she'd ever experienced. Soft one minute, intensely passionate the next. Strong, driving needs appeared out of nowhere. Instincts she didn't know she possessed tempted her. Without thought she tunneled her fingers into the hair at his nape and pressed herself against him, enjoying the sensation of touching so intimately.

But it didn't seem to be enough for Grant. Even as his mouth plundered hers, he tightened his hand around her waist and forced her even more snugly against him. His other hand went to her neck, sending a shaft of icy fire down her spine and directing her head into a position that gave him greater access to her mouth.

Kristen didn't care. She reveled in the hunger he created in her and rejoiced in the desire she obviously created in him. She never felt such pounding need, never felt such complete vulnerability to another person, even as she experienced a surge of power and control over him. She knew she'd stepped over a line, crossed a boundary that she'd never crossed before, and most of her didn't care, but part of her panicked. Not because she shared an overwhelming lust with a man who was supposed to be off limits to her, but because she'd never shared these feelings, these sensations, with Bradley. And she'd certainly never felt the power.

Shocked, ashamed, she jerked away.

For a good ten seconds they only stared at each other. Kristen saw her own astonishment mirrored in Grant's eyes, but she didn't see the shame or the confusion.

"Now, try to tell me you don't find me attractive," he said quietly into the absolutely silent room.

"I think we both pretty much know that I do."

Grant didn't realize he was holding his breath, waiting for her answer, until her hushed words fully penetrated his brain. Then he struggled to keep from sighing with relief. But one of the things that kept him from having any sense of relief at all was the regret he saw in her eyes. He would have cursed himself for pushing her this hard, this far, except he was very glad to have all this out in the open. He didn't want to have to deal with another employee who disliked him, and certainly didn't want an employee who disliked him caring for his babies. But he could deal with a physical attraction to her and he believed she could deal with a physical attraction to him. Mature, honest, sensible adults could even enjoy it. He *intended* to enjoy it.

"Okay, then. Why do I see such regret in your eyes?"

She took her time answering him. She fiddled with the silverware for at least a minute. But Grant didn't push her. He recognized deep, important feelings shining through her green eyes. But he also felt that whatever her problem, he could solve it.

"I dated my husband for four years and was married to him for three." She paused, caught his gaze. "But I never felt anything this powerful."

Astounded, he stared at her. "Kristen, you were with him seven years?"

She nodded. "I met Bradley when I was sixteen and married him at twenty."

"When I was twenty I was seeing three women and raising hell in bars where I wasn't even old enough to drink yet."

Reminded of their differences, Kristen swallowed hard. No matter how explosive the chemistry between them, their worlds were miles apart. No matter that she'd had her own rebellious streak at one time. She was currently a quiet, serious woman. He was a hell-raiser with no intention of settling down. He'd told her as much during dinner.

"Yeah, well, I knew I was in love at seventeen and I'd say I was fully settled at eighteen. I'm not turning back the maturity clock for anyone."

As Kristen watched anger grow in Grant's eyes because she called him immature, he continued to stare at her. When he spoke it was with menacing quiet. "I'd never be so arrogant as to mistake boredom for maturity and spiritedness for immaturity, but I will respect your wishes. If you want me to stay away from you I will."

He turned to walk out of the room and Kristen felt strangely disappointed, yet somehow vindicated. If what he felt for her was truly strong and good, he wouldn't have been so easily dissuaded.

Chapter Seven

"I think I need to tell him the truth," Kristen said to Mrs. Romani the next morning as she fed Taylor, and Mrs. Romani held Annie loosely in her arms and polka-danced around the kitchen.

Mrs. Romani stopped dancing. "No. Absolutely no."

"You didn't see the way he was looking at me last night."

"No, I didn't see the way he was looking at you last night," Mrs. Romani agreed, grinning. "But I made some powerful guesses in my head."

"This isn't funny!" Kristen gasped. "I don't have a clue what's going on between us, but I do know it's not helping the cause."

"It might not be hurting it, either," Mrs. Romani suggested, then began to glide around the kitchen with the giggling baby girl in her arms. Dressed in a flowing pink robe and wearing pink spongy curlers, Mrs. Romani looked comical on her own, but holding the bouncing, happy ten-

month-old baby and dancing around the kitchen, she looked
utterly ridiculous. But Annie was happy. Really happy.

And that struck Kristen in the oddest way.

She hadn't missed noticing that Grant would go to great
lengths to make sure that the children were well cared for,
even to the point of making the nanny happy. He tolerated
a housekeeper he less than adored, and paid her well because she was very good at what she did, and as far as he
was concerned, that was what mattered. As if all that wasn't
enough, he bathed, diapered and fed the children because
he didn't believe in discharging their care completely to
strangers. These kids were his duty and he took his responsibilities to the limit, with great results: the triplets were the
happiest babies Kristen had ever seen.

As that thought formed, Grant pushed open the swinging
door to the kitchen almost exactly the same time the back
door opened bringing Evan and Claire with Cody.

Caught, Mrs. Romani froze middance step in front of the
stove. Grant crossed his arms on his chest. "Well, now. Isn't
this interesting."

"I was just holding Annie to keep her from crying while
Kristen fed Taylor."

"You were dancing," Grant said, as if it were an accu-
sation.

Mrs. Romani glared at him. "I was keeping her from
crying."

"You were *playing* with her."

"It's not a crime," Evan said, jumping into the conversation.

"No, but she's tried to make me believe she doesn't like
these kids," Grant said, pointing his finger at Mrs. Romani
as he strode to the stove for coffee. "And I think I finally
figured out why."

Wide-eyed and curious, the other four adults in the room all said, "Why?"

"Because she thinks I'll dump extra work on her if I know she likes the kids."

Mrs. Romani glared at him again. "Actually, Grant, it's because you're such a nitpicker. I didn't want the aggravation of getting criticized every time one of the kids hiccuped wrong."

"I'm not a nitpicker!" Grant gasped.

"You're a nitpicker," Evan contradicted.

Grant looked to Kristen for help with his argument but the second their eyes met, the rest of the room disappeared for her. She felt the power of their kiss last night as fully and completely as if their lips were still touching. Her blood heated. Her limbs went numb. Even her breathing hitched.

Grant broke the spell by turning away without getting an answer. "I have meetings at the site in about an hour," he said, completely dismissing the prior conversation. "Is everyone set for this morning?"

"We're fine," Kristen managed to answer quietly.

Mrs. Romani's chin lifted. "Yeah, we're fine."

Grant turned and gave her a curt stare. "No kidding."

But even as Grant strode out the back door of the kitchen to the garage, carrying his steaming mug of coffee, Kristen realized he wasn't angry that Mrs. Romani had fooled him all these months, but pleased that she truly loved his kids. Since he wasn't the kind to stand around and participate in sentimentality and Mrs. Romani wasn't the kind to gush over anyone, a sarcastic comment was as close as they would come to agreeing she would now join in the care of the children.

"That went well," Evan observed, rolling his eyes as he walked to the coffeepot.

Kristen laughed. "Actually it went very well."

Mrs. Romani harrumphed as she walked to the stove. "Anybody want breakfast?" she asked casually.

Claire and Evan happily took her up on the offer of bacon and eggs, but Kristen shook her head, refusing to let Mrs. Romani off the hook this easily. "You and Grant just made an agreement that you would now start caring for the kids, or at least picking up the slack."

Cracking an egg on a skillet, Mrs. Romani shrugged. "So?"

"So, don't you go acting like nothing happened," Kristen said, but she giggled. "You two *like* each other."

Mrs. Romani ignored her, but Claire gasped with understanding. "I saw it, too. I think you pretend not to like each other."

Confused, Evan looked at all three women. "Why?"

"Because they are both stubborn," Kirsten said. "Neither wants to admit they're giving an inch, so they pretend nothing happened. But lots happened. In fact, I think this has been coming around for a couple of days."

"Maybe since you've been here," Claire said, taking a seat at the kitchen table. Cheerful, Cody slapped his hands on the table.

Kristen shook her head. "I didn't have anything to do with it."

"Don't be so sure," Evan disagreed. "Thinking about it, I can see Grant has been a tad more mellow."

"No, not mellow," Claire said, pondering as she spoke. "I think it's more like relaxed." She paused and caught Kristen's gaze. "Because he really trusts you," she added as Mrs. Romani placed a plate of eggs and toast in front of her.

Two things struck Kristen. First, this was a wonderful family. Even the nutty housekeeper fit. She handled Grant, she pampered the babies, she cared for Evan and Claire and

even counseled Kristen. Second, Grant shouldn't trust her.
Darn it! She was here under false pretenses. Yes, she was
trying to gain his confidence and respect and to prove that
she was a normal, caring person, but if she didn't soon explain who she was, everything she accomplished would go
flying out the window.

Kristen decided that Claire's opinion that Grant trusted
her was a sign that she had fulfilled her goal as much as it
could be fulfilled without admitting who she was. Until she
told Grant she was Angela's sister she could go no further
in this household. Still, she waited for Evan and Claire to
leave before she allowed her plan to fully form.

"Mrs. Romani," she said, spooning some oatmeal into
Taylor's open mouth. "Could I ask a favor?"

"Sure."

"I think I'd like to make dinner for me and Grant tonight."

Mrs. Romani's eyebrows rose.

"Now, don't go there," Kristen protested. "This is serious. This morning I saw things I'd never seen before."

Marian Romani gave her a puzzled look. "Like what?"

"Like each and every one of you plays a really important
role in caring for these kids, except me." She paused, gathering her thoughts. "I'm the kids' aunt, yet I'm the outsider."

For the first time in a long time, Mrs. Romani turned
serious, even sentimental. "You're not an outsider. You're
very important here, too."

"Yes and no. If I really were a nanny, what I'm doing
with these kids would be wonderful. But since I'm their
aunt, and since no one knows that but you and me and the
kids, things aren't happening the way they should be."

"Exactly how do you think they should be happening?"

Kristen raised her eyes to look at Mrs. Romani, knowing

l her guilt was visible in them. "Maybe the Brewsters ouldn't be so nice to me."

"Oh, honey, they'd be nice to you," Mrs. Romani con-led, putting her hand on Kristen's shoulder. "Just like rant accepted me this morning, now that they know you en't a threat, they're going to welcome you into their fam-y with open arms."

Kristen wished she could believe that. But there were two ings wrong with Mrs. Romani's assumptions. First, though rant had accepted Mrs. Romani, the situations were en-rely different. Mrs. Romani hid the fact that she adored e kids. Kristen hid an important piece of information. omething that would impact everybody's life.

Second, Kristen wasn't entirely sure she wasn't a threat. he still wanted the ranch. She still wanted the chance to aise these kids. If she and Grant couldn't come up with a uitable compromise, she couldn't promise she wouldn't ke this wonderful, loving family to court and try to get e babies away from them.

Grant arrived home from work later than usual that eve-ing. Because he had called ahead and told everyone of his lans, he didn't think it would be a problem. Particularly nce Evan and Claire had decided to take the children to e mall that night. Somehow or another Grant had missed e fact that Thanksgiving was only a few days away, and hristmas was just around the corner. This would be their rst Christmas with the kids. His first Christmas as a father. nd the Brewsters' first Christmas as a family in years.

It filled him with sadness and guilt to realize that he'd gnored the last two years of his father's life. But caring for e triplets eased some of the guilt because he could almost el his father's approval. And with that approval he felt rgiveness. It had taken months for everything to sink in and months for him to learn how to care for the kids and to run the empire his family was building, but finally everything was falling into place.

Except for Kristen.

He had no idea what her place should be in his life. He'd told her the night before that no woman had ever made him think about marriage, but he'd lied. *She* had made him think about marriage. But it was wrong. Dead wrong. Not only was she too young for him, but she arrived at a point in his life when he was lonely. He couldn't help but wonder if the coincidence made him see things that weren't really there. Even though Kristen answered his kiss the night before with unbridled passion, it wasn't passion she wanted to feel. And that was really the bottom line. If she didn't want to feel it, then there were good reasons. Probably the same reasons he saw. She was too young for him, and she was still coming to terms with being widowed. Add those to the very real truth that he was suddenly a lonely man longing for company, and he could certainly understand how anybody might think this situation didn't work. God knew he thought it himself.

If Kristen Devereaux didn't want to have anything to do with him, he sure as hell didn't blame her.

He walked through the front door and the wonderful aroma of chicken greeted him. He couldn't remember the last time he ate and the enticing scent pulled him through the foyer, down the hall and to the kitchen.

The empty kitchen.

"Mrs. Romani...Kristen..." he called, roaming through the all-white room around the corner to the alcove, which led to Mrs. Romani's quarters. Her door was wide-open, but the lights were off, indicating she wasn't around.

"She went with Evan and Claire to take the kids to the

mall,'' Kristen said from behind and Grant spun around to face her.

Then almost wished he hadn't. Looking at the beautiful picture she made standing beyond the butcher block, dressed in an outfit he'd once heard his mother describe as lounging pajamas, Grant felt reactions he knew were illegal in at least three Southern states.

Despite the modesty of her attire, the floral print of blue, pink and beige reminded him that she was a soft, warm, receptive woman, which reminded him that he liked her very much. His feelings for Kristen were primarily physical, but he didn't discount the way he could talk to her, the way she could get him to say things he'd never told anyone else, and even the way he could relax with her. Be himself with her.

''Hi.''

''Hi,'' she casually replied, then walked over to the stove. She opened the oven and pulled out a well-roasted chicken. ''Don't let the color fool you,'' she said, nodding to the bird, which was a little browner than normal. ''It's perfect.''

''Okay,'' he said, then loosened his tie. The room was incredibly warm and all his senses were on red alert. Recognizing she'd dressed in a beautiful outfit when they were alone didn't help matters much. Both had his mind rolling in all kinds of directions it shouldn't be rolling.

He shrugged out of his jacket. ''I hope we can eat right now because I'm starved...and tired,'' he added, striving to alleviate any fear she might have that he would make a pass at her this evening.

She lifted her eyes until her gaze met his. ''I hope you're not *too* tired because I think we need to talk...while we have the house to ourselves.''

Okay. Now *that* one he hadn't misinterpreted. That was direct and official. There was only one reason a man and a woman needed a house to themselves. She wanted them to become lovers. Apparently she'd thought over everything that had happened the night before and everything that had been happening to them since they'd met. She'd considered their differences. She'd considered their life problems.

And she still wanted to be his lover.

The thought alone warmed him all over, and aroused him so entirely that he could have taken her right there, in the kitchen, without regard for anything but slaking this pounding lust that had been driving him crazy. But, at the same time, the knowledge humbled him. This was a strong, but vulnerable, woman. For her, the decision to become someone's lover would not be an easy one. Nor one entered into lightly.

This was a significant moment in her life, which meant he had to make it special, meaningful.

There really wasn't a quick, easy way to confess to someone that you were in his home under false pretenses. Emily Post certainly didn't have a book on it. Oprah hadn't yet done that show. And Grant treating Kristen as if she were the most important woman is his life just made things even more difficult.

Under normal circumstances, he was a gorgeous, intelligent man with worthwhile opinions, a strong sense of family, an integrity that went beyond most people's understanding and sex appeal that could knock the socks off a woman wearing tennis shoes. But tonight he'd pulled out all the stops. If she'd hoped he'd be polite, he went past polite the whole way to solicitous. He laughed at her stories about the kids, hung on her every word and held her gaze as if everything she said was of such a momentous consequence he didn't want to miss a thing.

Somehow she managed to get through dinner without falling at his feet in adoration, but she also hadn't told him the truth about herself. She decided that was because memories of the kiss from last night lingered in the air of the dining room, complicating things even further. She needed to get them into a different room, where she could regain her perspective and her sanity, and she would stop thinking about things like how beautiful his eyes were, or how sexy his smile was, or even how nicely they seemed to blend together.

"Dinner was wonderful," Grant said, bringing Kristen out of her thoughts. But when he placed his hand atop hers and set off a chain reaction of spiraling tingles from her fingertips to her toes, she knew her thinking had been correct. She had to move them to a different location.

"How about if we have our coffee in the family room?"

Somehow or another her suggestion didn't have the effect on him that she'd expected. Instead of breaking the spell being woven around them, her suggestion seemed to make things worse. His dark eyes became smoky and seductive. His smile became provocative, enticing, playing tricks with her nervous system.

Just when she might have changed her mind and asked to stay right where she was, he rose and took her hand. Before urging her to stand, however, he brought the tips of her fingers to his lips and kissed each one individually.

Kristen fought the warm sensations that flowed through her. Her knees weakened so quickly she almost swooned. Her head swam. If he hadn't given the light tug that started her legs moving, she knew she might have fainted.

But the walk to the family room provided sanity and clarity. Obviously he had this all wrong. He might have kept her head clouded sufficiently through dinner so that she hadn't recognized that he thought this private dinner meant much more than she intended, but now that dinner was over and now that walking had blood flowing to her brain again, she could tell his misinterpretation was their problem.

A few sentences would allow her to straighten this all out, and immediately on the heels of that she planned to confess who she was. It wasn't the most pleasant way to handle things and given the choice she probably would have picked an atmosphere a lot less charged with sexual energy. But with the rate things kept happening between them—heck, with the very fact that things kept happening between them—Kristen realized her choices were quickly being taken away from her.

"I think you have the wrong impression, here," Kristen said as she and Grant sat on the sofa together.

"Really?" he asked, smiling at her.

Damn him, Kristen thought, wishing she could inch away, but for some reason or another unable to do so. His dark eyes held her captive. The arm he'd casually placed across the back of the sofa just inches away from her neck beckoned to her to lean into him. She held herself rigid and stiff.

After clearing her throat, she said, "There are things we need to talk about."

"I know."

She ventured another look into his eyes. "Big things. Important things."

He nodded, but the fingers that had been a fairly safe distance away were suddenly on the back of her neck, stroking lightly. Even as she felt herself being lulled into a comfortable, relaxed state, arousal danced in the pit of her stomach.

Not good.

"Grant, please," she whispered.

"Please what?"

"Oh, no," she said, stifling the urge to jump and run. She couldn't jump and run. She couldn't show weakness.

She had to be strong and she had to do this. "Let's not get into those silly little word games with each other—"

"You're right," he said before she could finish her sentence. His fingers tightened ever so slightly on her neck to pull her forward. "I think there have been enough games between us."

He kissed her so quickly and so thoroughly that Kristen didn't have time to think, only react. The arms she'd held stiffly at her sides came up around him. The mouth that had been so desperate to confess the truth, opened to him, allowing him access, kissing him back. The fingers that itched to touch him did exactly that. They became restless, greedy.

And the more driven and ambitious she became, the more he challenged her. With his hands and his mouth, he took them higher and higher until the very world in which they existed began to disappear. Even as she felt every move he made, every sensation those moves created in her body, she felt herself falling into a velvet tunnel of perception where thoughts and feelings seemed to mix and mingle until they became one.

And everything else in the world disappeared. She wasn't alone and lonely. Desperate for company. Longing for love. There were no troubles and problems. Just yearnings and needs and someone who shared both. Someone who wanted her as much as she wanted him.

With her palms pressed against his cheeks, Kristen deepened the kiss, poured herself, her needs, into every move she made, sharing her vulnerability, expressing her hope, while his hands raced over her back and up her waist until they greedily filled themselves with her breasts.

The burst of arousal created by that one touch weakened her to the point that she nearly whimpered. He seemed to sense that, and drew her back, slowing the kiss, soothing her with soft strokes and whispered words.

But by now Kristen was trembling with desire, and where a few minutes ago desire had clouded her thoughts this time it unexpectedly cleared them. And tears sprang to her eyes.

She was on a sofa with a man she barely knew, ready to give him everything she owned—the only thing she really owned—herself. She'd allowed him to take her to a place they really shouldn't go and ruined her well-planned opportunity to confess the truth, but more than that, in her shamelessness, she'd defamed Bradley's memory.

Shaking, confused, more hurt than she cared to admit, Kristen pulled herself away. "I have to leave now."

He could tell from the quiver in her voice that there would be no changing her mind, but also knew neither one of them had misinterpreted anything. They wanted each other. She might need another day or two to acclimate herself to the fact that they'd reached a point where there was no turning back, but she would accept it—if only because she wanted it as much as he did.

Before she could rise, he caught her hand. "I'll see you in the morning," he whispered, then lightly brushed his lips across her knuckles. Everything about her was perfect. Soft and feminine. Delicate yet strong. He'd never met a woman who could complement him *and* arouse him. Women had been his equal. Women had made him weak with longing. But only this woman had done both.

He would not let her get away. No matter how much she thought she wanted to.

Chapter Eight

Tossing and turning in her bed that night, Kristen decided that for Grant to so easily get her off the path of her mission, she had to have stronger feelings for him than merely sexual. The funny part of it was she could understand, forgive herself, if her feelings for Grant were nothing but physical longings. After all, he was an incredibly attractive man and she was a normal woman. But the truth was every day she found herself caring more and more about him. Wanting to help him. Wanting to understand him. Wanting to let herself be the woman she knew he knew she could be for him because she saw it in his eyes.

The truth was the vision of herself she saw in his eyes was very tempting. She *wanted* to step into the role he seemed to have created for her.

She wanted to be more than his lover. She wanted to be his friend, his companion, his *confidante*. Just as he wanted her to be. But it was wrong. Wrong. Wrong. Wrong. Her husband had been gone only fourteen months and she was ready to replace him with a man she'd known about twelve days.

It was wrong.

That was the last thought she had as she drifted off to sleep that night and the first thought she had when she awakened, until she realized that it wasn't the sound of a baby crying that had brought her from slumber, but a light, clandestine knock.

"Who is it?" she mumbled, her mind still fuzzy with sleep.

"It's me," Mrs. Romani whispered, then let herself into Kristen's room.

"Mrs. Romani?" Kristen said, totally confused.

"Get yourself out of bed," Marian said, yanking back Kristen's covers. "Grant's already up. He's got both the girls dressed and he's feeding them." She said the last as she tugged Kristen out of bed and directed her toward her bathroom. "You didn't tell him last night, did you?"

Kristen shook her head.

"I didn't think so. He's whistling."

"Oh, no," Kristen said and sank to her bed again. "That's awful."

"It's awful that he's happy?" Mrs. Romani asked, confused.

"Yes!" Kristen said, raising her pleading eyes to the puzzled housekeeper.

"Oh, no," Mrs. Romani said and joined Kristen on her bed. "He kissed you, didn't he?"

"He did more than kiss me," Kristen mumbled. Gathering her courage and her robe, she headed for her bathroom. "But I'm sure after I tell him who I am this morning, he won't kiss me again."

"This is the first time I've seen that man happy in the

three months I've been here and you're going to burst his bubble?''

"I have to burst his bubble,'' Kristen said, staring at Mrs. Romani. "You seem to forget that what I have to tell him has some very important consequences.''

"You could work around that.''

"Work around it?'' Kristen asked, stupefied. "Don't you see that if I don't soon tell him who I am, he's going to think I was deliberately keeping it from him?''

"In some ways you were,'' Mrs. Romani said. "But for good reason. You wanted to find out if these guys were the appropriate caretakers for your sister's kids. You couldn't come right out and ask them, so you made a logical choice. It's not a crime. And you're not a criminal, just someone who wanted to know all the facts before she showed her own hand,'' she said, and opened the bedroom door. "I'll see you downstairs.''

Her mood improved by Mrs. Romani's rationalization, Kristen didn't waste too much time getting her shower. Though she did take a little more care than usual with how she looked. No matter what happened and kept happening between her and Grant, she was the children's aunt and she needed to make a good impression. She also needed to ask for help getting the ranch and finding a way to be a part of the children's lives. She now recognized that she wouldn't get permanent custody of the children. Truth be known, she didn't believe it would be proper for her to take the kids from people who loved them and cared for them very well. But she did want the ranch back in her family and she did want to be a part of the children's lives. Knowing everything she knew about Grant, she genuinely believed he would help her.

But only if she presented her request in the right way. If she waited one more day, or let things go any further be-

tween them without admitting who she was, he wouldn't
trust her. She'd ruin everything she'd worked so hard to put
together in the past two weeks.

She decided to talk with him at breakfast when Mrs. Romani snuck outside or into the laundry room for her morning
cigarette, but the very second she set foot in the kitchen,
Claire entered through the back door, with Evan right behind her, carrying Cody.

She glanced at the happy couple who had just entered,
bringing with them a gust of blustery November air, then at
Grant who was sitting at the table in front of the girls' high
chairs. He smiled at her and her stomach sank, her knees
liquefied.

"Bring that big boy over here," Mrs. Romani said, no
longer shy about her affection for the kids. "I'll get him out
of his jacket."

"Thanks," Claire said. After handing the baby to the
housekeeper, she began unbuttoning her wool coat. "I hope
you have coffee."

"Plenty of coffee," Mrs. Romani said, but Kristen didn't
really pay any attention to what was happening around her.
She was caught in Grant's hypnotic gaze. It amazed her,
thrilled her and scared the devil out of her that he could say
so much, and make her feel so much just with the way he
looked at her.

"How about you, honey, coffee?"

Mrs. Romani's question penetrated Kristen's muddled
state. As it did, the sounds of two baby girls screeching and
whining for attention, the clank and clatter of cups and
spoons being removed from the cabinets, and Cody's giggling also managed to push their way into Kristen's brain.
She wondered how long she'd stood frozen, staring at Grant
like a lovesick puppy, then decided it didn't matter. He'd
been staring at her, too. They'd been staring at each other.

And if they didn't soon stop, everybody was going to notice.

She cleared her throat and walked over to the stove. "I'd love some coffee, but I'll get it myself. Since you have Cody, maybe I should pour you some?"

"I can handle pouring coffee with a baby on my hip," Mrs. Romani said, but nonetheless took a seat at the round wooden table. Having gotten his own coffee, Evan sat beside her and Claire leaned against the counter. They were one big, joyous family, and somehow or another Kristen had managed to wrangle her way into it.

As Kristen set Mrs. Romani's coffee on the table, a hot surge of guilt poured through her. Under false pretenses, she'd made good friends, she'd earned everyone's trust, and she was falling in love with the family patriarch.

This had to stop.

"Grant," she said, then cleared her throat again. "Since the kids all seem settled, would it be possible for us to have a minute in the den?"

He looked at his watch. "Actually, Kristen, I'm running late. I'm supposed to be at a meeting in five minutes and it will take me ten just to drive to town."

With her very position in this happy household at stake, Kristen knew she couldn't wait. She captured his gaze and held it, hoping to convey the urgency. "This is really important."

He glanced at his watch again. "Okay. Two minutes," he said, then he smiled at her as he rose and indicated that she should precede him to the den.

She didn't say anything as they walked. Neither did he. When they reached the den, she closed the door behind them, but as she turned around to face him, he caught her by the waist, hauled her against him and kissed her soundly enough to weaken her knees and turn her brain to absolute mush.

But, bracing her hands against his broad shoulders for support, Kristen was suddenly jolted by a flash of insight that left her almost as weak as his ardent kiss. The biggest difference between Bradley and Grant was temperament. Bradley was sweet and shy. Grant was not. He didn't hesitate to go after what he wanted. She'd always assumed the contrast was a matter of personality, but this morning Kristen was beginning to wonder if it wasn't something of a maturity issue. Bradley Devereaux was a boy, still finding his way into his life, still struggling for his experience and seasoning. On that journey with him, Kristen felt safe and secure, because she was struggling to find herself as well.

But Grant Brewster was a man. He wasn't struggling to discover who he was. He didn't need any more seasoning. He was who he was supposed to be.

Bradley Devereaux had been the boy of her dreams when she was a teenager but now that she'd suffered through losing him, through learning to live without him, she wasn't a girl anymore. She was a woman. And she needed an entirely different kind of mate. She needed someone as strong and sure of himself as Grant was. By falling in love with Grant, she wasn't belittling Bradley's memory, or even intimating that he had not been the love of her life, she was simply keeping up with the changes that had occurred in her.

And that was why she continually got confused. That was why she kept forgetting why it was wrong to be with somebody like Grant. Because it wasn't wrong. It was right. Absolutely right. Almost as if they were made for each other.

"I've been wanting to do that from the second you walked through the kitchen door," Grant said, breaking the kiss, leaving her breathless and befuddled. He reached for his briefcase. "I'm glad you thought up an excuse. But I really do have to run."

He gave her another quick peck on the lips, then strode to the door. Her mind still on the realization that her life had shifted, her thinking had shifted...*she* had shifted and grown enough that she had become the woman Grant Brewster needed, she only stared at him. By the time she collected her wits and recognized he'd thought she only coerced him into the den for a kiss, she groaned with desperation then began to run after him. "Grant! No," she said. "I really need to talk with you."

The end of her sentence was punctuated by the sound of the front door clicking shut and Kristen stopped dead in her tracks, staring at the polished wood and stained glass. The man was going to kill her with sexual energy. She was sure. He made her feel weak and wonderful and at the same time supercharged with the need to do things that went so far beyond the boundaries of what she'd done with Bradley that she had been forced to understand and sort out her feelings this morning or think she was crazy. Now, at least, she recognized that she was perfectly normal. And falling for Grant was normal. When she talked with him, there wouldn't be any confusion in her. When she admitted to being the triplets' aunt, she could also admit she was falling head over heels in love with him. She wouldn't have to run scared anymore...because she wasn't scared anymore.

But in the silence of the front hall, sadness filled her.

She didn't *want* to forget Bradley.

Though she knew she had to press into the future, a part of her hated that the only way she could do that was by letting go of the past.

Whistling as he drove to the diner to meet Evan for lunch that afternoon, Grant realized he had never met anyone like

Kristen. No woman had ever made him feel the things she made him feel. Not just the sexual things, but also a myriad of other emotions of which he'd thought himself incapable. Recognizing that she was the first person with whom he could leave the children and not worry the entire time he was gone, Grant knew that she'd worked her way into his trust.

And that wasn't just astounding. Grant counted it as something of a miracle.

"Busy morning?" Evan asked, grinning as Grant slid onto the bench seat across from his brother.

Puzzled, Grant frowned at his brother. Either Evan didn't know Arnie Garrett was sitting in the booth behind him, or he'd made peace with the fact that their father's former attorney had accused them of being unable to care for the kids, because Evan didn't seem nervous or angry.

"Extremely. Now, what's so important that we needed to meet?" He paused, glanced around and, taking his cue from Evan, grew comfortable himself. Brewster County was a full-fledged county but it was populated with more trees than people, and because of that it had only one real town, Brewster. Since Arnie Garrett had been the town's only attorney for decades, he was a fixture in the community, and Grant knew they couldn't avoid or ignore the man forever. He didn't feel ready to forgive him for insinuating the Brewsters couldn't handle raising the triplets, but he knew they still had to live in the same community and that eventually they might even work together. If growing accustomed to him meant being able to sit near him in the diner without wanting to punch him, then Grant knew he had to do it.

"And where's Claire?"

"I left her at the office because I wanted to talk with you privately."

Grant only stared at him. "About what? What can't you talk about in front of Claire?"

"Absolutely nothing. Claire and I don't have secrets. I don't have anything to hide," he said, then sipped his coffee. "Unfortunately, I'm afraid you do."

"Me?" Grant gasped.

"Don't play coy, Grant," Evan said with a chuckle. "You can't pull it off. Just like you and Kristen weren't fooling anyone with that trip to the den this morning. You went back there to kiss."

"What!"

Evan looked him right in the eye. "Are you denying it?"

To his great astonishment and horror, Grant felt his face heat with color.

"Caught you."

"All right. Damn it," Grant said, then signaled the waitress to bring him coffee. When she was gone, he felt a little more in control of his emotions and he sighed. This appeared to be his morning of reckoning. First, he'd admitted to himself that he liked Kristen more than he thought. Then he let Arnie Garrett sit close enough to spit on without going ballistic. Now he was realizing it might be time to get others adjusted to his unusual feelings for Kristen.

He decided it might not be a bad thing that his brother had picked up on the fact that he and Kristen were more than housemates. Because he'd never had these kinds of feelings before, because he didn't know where they would take him, because he did envy the relationships his brothers had, Grant couldn't pretend nothing was happening. Not only was he a man feeling his way down a blind alley, bound to make some awkward mistakes, but he wanted everything life with Kristen seemed to be offering.

But he also needed to be careful, cautious. He hadn't even talked with Kristen yet about his feelings, so he couldn't exactly blurt everything to his brother—though it was time he started admitting the obvious.

"We seem to be growing a little close."

"That's what has me and Claire worried," Evan said, studying his brother.

Under the scrutiny, Grant fought the urge to squirm in his seat. Even before Evan made his next comments, Grant knew why he was so fidgety and why Evan had chosen to talk with him.

"You're not known for your fidelity, Grant."

"I've never been *un*faithful," Grant countered with a grin, trying to lighten the mood.

"No, not by the strictest definition of the word because you've never given a woman a commitment."

"Maybe this time is different," Grant suggested nonchalantly, not just to keep the mood intact, but also because this really wasn't any of Evan's business. Not yet, anyway. As far as he and Kristen were concerned, this was still the planning stages. He couldn't make any promises. He shouldn't have to.

"And maybe it's not."

"And maybe it's none of your business."

Evan shook his head. "Anything to do with those triplets is my business," Evan reminded firmly. "I don't give a flying fig about your love life, Grant, but I can see that Kristen Devereaux is a sweet, shy young woman who doesn't deserve to get her heart broken."

"Well, thank you for the vote of confidence."

"I'm not trying to be critical, I'm just trying to look out for the kids. If you break her heart, she's going to leave, and then where will we be? Up the creek without a nanny, that's where," Evan stated emphatically. "I don't give a damn if you horse around with every woman from here to Ohio. But if you hurt this woman and she leaves, you won't just deal with me and Claire, you'll also be back to square one with three babies who fell in love with her so quickly you'd swear she was the one related to them instead of us.''

Put off by being taken to task by his younger brother, particularly since Evan was way, way off base, Grant desperately wanted to ignore him, but he couldn't. For as much off base as he was, Evan also had some good points.

"All right," he said, then again hailed the waitress. "I'll behave.''

But even as he made the promise, Grant didn't know how he was going to keep it. Since he hadn't been able to keep his hands off her for the twelve days she'd lived in his house, it seemed a fairly safe bet he wouldn't be able to keep his hands off her in the future.

Still shaken, Kristen threw herself into playing with the kids. Busy with laundry and housecleaning, Mrs. Romani couldn't give her any help, but Kristen didn't care. She needed three energetic kids to keep her mind occupied. But Kristen also had to concede that when they ate an early lunch at eleven and immediately wanted to nap, she was grateful for the break.

Jogging down the spiral stairway, searching for a way to keep herself from thinking about Bradley or Grant for the two hours the children would sleep, she was jolted out of her reverie by the ringing phone.

Knowing Mrs. Romani was probably up to her elbows in cleanser, Kristen automatically answered it. "Brewster residence.''

"Kristen?''

Not recognizing the voice on the other end of the line, Kristen said, "Yes? Who is this?''

"I'm sorry. I didn't mean to be impolite. My name is Arnie Garrett, I represented Norm Brewster before he died, but I also wrote to you about withdrawing from your sister's claim for the Morris ranch.''

"Yes,'' Kristen said, sighing with acknowledgment. "I'm sorry. Was I supposed to answer that letter?''

Arnie Garrett laughed. "No. No. Informing you was nothing more than a formality. But now that you're in town, I thought you might want to get together to talk about filing a claim for the ranch yourself.''

Kristen's forehead furrowed. Though her immediate response was positive—she would like to get an attorney's viewpoint of her chances for getting the ranch—it struck her as unusual that Arnie Garrett not only knew she was in Brewster, but he knew exactly where she was.

On the heels of that, she realized that if this man had been Norm Brewster's attorney, and if he had also made Angela's claim for the ranch, it was strange that he hadn't simply continued that claim for the triplets.

After all, *they* were Angela's heirs, not Kristen's.

"I don't think I have a claim for the ranch.''

"Well, you probably don't,'' Arnie admitted. "But the triplets do.''

"Then shouldn't you be talking with Evan, Grant or Chas?''

"I'd rather talk with you.''

"But that doesn't make any sense.''

"Look, sugar, I don't want to get pushy, but you're in no position to question me. I sat beside the Brewsters at lunch this afternoon and it seems to me they don't have a clue you're Angela's sister.''

By the time Grant arrived home that afternoon, he'd figured out how he would handle Evan and Claire's objections to his pursuing Kristen.

He would simply ask her to marry him.

Since the thought alone filled him with happiness and joy, then tossed him into a state of acute arousal, Grant decided it had to be right. True, they'd only met a two weeks ago, and, true, there were still many, many things they probably didn't know about each other. But in his heart Grant believed he knew everything that mattered. She was strong, smart, sweet and sexy. Dedicated, loyal, honest and fair. Good with his kids, friendly with his family, and driving him absolutely nuts with lust.

If there was anything else to learn about her, he considered it certifiably second to all of the above.

Besides, Evan had a point about securing Kristen's place in their lives. As it stood right now, Evan and Claire were needed at the mill. They didn't have time to care for the kids. When he returned from his honeymoon, Chas needed all his time for his law practice, and Lily had made plans to enroll in real estate classes. Grant himself should be working night and day, and finding Kristen Devereaux had been a real godsend. She fit the same way Claire had fit, the same way Lily had fit, but there was more. She loved the kids and *wanted* to be their caretaker. She didn't seem to have an ambition beyond the life Grant could offer her. And, in fact, she almost seemed to have been tailor-made to fill this role. If they were securing her place, it wasn't merely one-sided.

He wanted her. She wanted him. And she wanted this life. It was a match made in heaven, and they should get married.

They would make a commitment, and finally, he would have some peace. Because that's what all the confusion had been about since Chas's wedding. He needed someone to love and in less than two weeks he had fallen wonderfully, blissfully in love. He would not throw that away and, in spite of Evan's misgivings, he would not hurt Kristen. For the rest of his life he intended to love and cherish her. He would shower her with gifts, lavish her with love and wake up with her every morning for the rest of his life.

So, it was her name he called when he entered the front foyer. "Kristen?"

No answer.

"Kristen?"

No answer again.

With the effect of a fist punching a hole in his gut came the sudden, sick feeling that something was terribly, terribly wrong.

Chapter Nine

"We're back here, Grant," Claire said and Grant's forehead furrowed in confusion as he walked to the family room.

"What's up?" he asked his sister-in-law, bending to lift Taylor into his arms.

Holding Annie on her lap as she rolled a ball to Cody, Claire smiled at Grant. "Kristen had some sort of emergency."

Grant felt his heart stop. "Is she sick?"

"No. No," Claire said, shaking her head. "She's fine. She just said something came up and she had to take care of it."

Relieved, Grant sank into a chair, trying not to curse himself for panicking. "That's good," he said.

Remembering his conversation with Evan at lunch, he nearly confided his intentions about Kristen to Claire, but knew Kristen should be the first one he talked with. So he kept his voice light, neutral. "I mean, I'm glad nothing's wrong because she's a miracle worker with the kids. I'd hate to lose her.''

"Then you'd better start giving her some time off," Claire said, eyeing him coolly. "Do you realize she's been here two weeks and she's hardly had two minutes to herself?"

"She's only been here twelve days," Grant said, then recognized he'd been counting. If he needed any more proof that he was a man over the edge, that one simple action provided it.

"You can't work a person day and night, Grant," Claire said, rising. "I think you and Evan ought to modify your schedule to give her two full days off every week and a few evenings. Otherwise, we really are going to lose her."

Even though Grant had no intention of losing Kristen, he felt a quick stab of pain thinking that he might. Which was ridiculous. Once he asked her to marry him, she would be here to stay. Still, even as his wife, she shouldn't be overworked, or underappreciated. In fact, if he didn't straighten out the schedule she might get the foolish idea that he was only marrying her to care for the kids.

Just considering the possibility that Kristen might think he only wanted her for her child care abilities, Grant got a sick feeling in the pit of his stomach. What if that's what she believed? What if he asked her to marry him and she thought he'd only asked because he wanted her to care for the triplets? What if she refused?

Grant calmed himself by deciding they would correct the nanny situation immediately. *Before* he popped the question. If he and Evan sat down tonight and fixed the schedule, he would have proof to show Kristen that he wasn't simply marrying her for the kids. Then the schedule could prevent Kristen from being overworked until they were ready to announce their plans...at which point he might even have to find another nanny.

At which point he *would* find another nanny, so there would be no mistaking his feelings for her.

But even with all that logic firmly in place, Grant couldn't shake the sensation that something was wrong. Kristen's sudden need to be out of the house was unusual, abnormal. He had a strong gut instinct that whatever had dragged her away was convincing enough, important enough that he really could lose her.

And with that strong gut instinct came a surge of pain so severe, it baffled him. He had no intention of losing her. But even if he did, he'd known this woman twelve days. How could it possibly hurt this much just *thinking* about losing her? How could he have such intense feelings after such a short time?

And how would he live without her, if she left?

What if she was gone already?

Kristen parked her car in the side lot of Mr. Garrett's law offices and snuck around to the front door. Though it was already dark, she slipped into the building quickly, trying to make sure no one would see her.

"Hello?" she called. Not only was there no receptionist at the front desk, but most of the lights were off. Those lamps that were burning were set on dim.

A short, gray-haired man appeared in the doorway behind the desk. "You must be Kristen," he said kindly, offering his hand to shake hers as he approached her. "I'm Arnie Garrett."

"Mr. Garrett," Kristen said, then automatically slid her hand down her skirt after shaking his. In person, he was even sleazier looking than he'd sounded on the phone. From the appearance of the office, Kristen surmised he had at one time been prosperous but now the furniture was old and worn. She couldn't tell if he'd decided not to upgrade because he'd be retiring shortly, or if he simply couldn't afford to replace the aging equipment.

Either way, the shabby furniture, coupled with the lack of light and the company of the peculiar old man, gave her the creeps.

"Let's go back to my office where we can talk," he suggested and directed her to walk toward a beam of light.

Kristen did as he instructed, grateful she'd be more comfortable in the brightly lit room, thinking maybe then he wouldn't look so sinister. But once she was seated on the soft leather chair and he was seated across from her, behind the obviously deteriorating wooden desk, Kristen knew her first impression wasn't wrong. Even in the light, there was something about the man she neither liked nor trusted.

"You know, Norm Brewster was a client of mine all my life."

Not knowing anything of the sort, but too afraid to contradict him, Kristen attempted a smile and nodded.

"When he died, I lost all the business from the lumber mill and now Chas Brewster is taking clients away, too."

"So, you want to pay the Brewsters back by bypassing them in the claim for the ranch?" Kristen asked curiously, not thinking that a very smart move at all.

"No. No, Ms. Devereaux," he said before he leaned back in his chair. "This is much bigger than a claim for the ranch. Norm and your sister, Angela, had appointed me guardian of the triplets."

Kristen couldn't help it, she gasped. "What?"

"In the event the Brewster brothers hadn't wanted the kids, they were to go to me."

She didn't like the way he was talking about the kids as if they were property. If she hadn't already decided she didn't trust the man, that in and of itself would have been enough to persuade her.

"But the Brewsters wanted the kids."

He nodded. "Very much, it seems." He paused, tapping his fingertips together. "But they're young. And not very stable."

"How can you say that?" Kristen asked, incredulous. "Not only are two of them now married—making them perfect guardians—but Grant's as stable and responsible as they come."

Arnie Garrett smiled evilly. "Oh, sure, as long as he's not chasing a woman or a bottle."

"I've never seen him drink."

"Yeah, and I'll bet you've never seen him chase a woman, either."

Her face flushed with color and Arnie Garrett grinned in surprise. "Well, I'll be damned. Looks like our third Brewster brother is playing fast and loose with a nanny."

"It's not like that at all."

"Oh, that's right. This would be true love. You've been there what? A week? Two? And he's got you convinced he loves you." Arnie smiled again. "He's very good, Ms. Devereaux. Don't ever forget that."

Angry now, Kristen glared at him. "What do you want, Mr. Garrett?"

All business, he sat forward. "I want your help to get those kids."

She shook her head. "Those kids are exactly where they belong."

"Oh, you mean you don't want to take them to Texas?"

Desperately. She wanted to take them to Texas desperately. If only because she felt she was deserting her heritage, her whole life, forgetting her past and the people who gave it meaning.

But there were stronger ties to keep the triplets here, and there might be stronger ties to keep *her* here.

"You know, Angela only married Norm to have a baby to get the ranch," Arnie said quietly, kindly. "And Norm only married Angela as something of a good deed."

Having assumed that much, Kristen nodded.

"And do you know why?"

Kristen shook her head.

"For you. They both did it for you."

Hearing that, Kristen's eyes filled with tears and she looked up sharply. "But she couldn't...she shouldn't."

"I know that and you know that," Arnie agreed, pointing across the desk at her. "But to hear Angela tell the story, after your husband died you were in the kind of depression that could last a lifetime. Losing the ranch would have been the final straw. She was worried about you."

Guilty, Kristen nodded. "I know."

"And she wanted *you* to have that ranch," he added quietly. "Didn't you meet your husband there?"

Kristen nodded again.

"It was where you lived when you were first married, too, right?"

She swallowed.

"Lot of memories there, I'll bet," Arnie said, tapping a pencil on his desk. "Good times with a good man. Not someone like Grant Brewster, Mr. Love-'em-and-leave-'em."

The comparison of her late husband with Grant actually made her shake, and she knew this was the conclusion she'd been trying to draw all along, but wouldn't let herself. A few passionate, mind-numbing kisses had blinded her to reality. Grant was seducing her. In his own house, at the risk of his children's care. He didn't give a damn if he hurt her. He didn't give a damn if the kids lost a good nanny.

All he thought about was himself.

And she'd almost given up Bradley and his memory for him.

"Together you and I could get that ranch."

Again, Kristen looked up sharply. She'd all but forgotten someone was in the room with her.

Arnie smiled "It would be very simple. Having lived in the household for almost two weeks, you could testify that the children are not being properly cared for. Custody would revert to me as alternate guardian appointed in the will, and I would get your ranch for you."

When the rain began to fall, Grant came as close to full-scale panic as he'd ever been in his life. Because of the overhanging clouds, the typically black sky became even blacker. Without any assistance from streetlights, the roads in this dense forest county were treacherous. High beams could penetrate the darkness, but being unfamiliar with the roads, Kristen would still need to drive with caution.

That is, if she was driving back. For all he knew, she'd driven through the storm and was on her way to parts unknown. He wouldn't blame her for leaving. He'd probably scared her. Hell, he'd scared himself.

"Grant, Claire said you and I have some business we need to discuss," Evan said as he entered the den, bringing Grant from his thoughts.

Blowing his breath out on a long sigh, Grant turned away from the window of the den. "Yeah. There are some things we need to discuss."

Rather than answer, Evan only studied Grant for a few seconds, then he shook his head. "I can't believe you're worried."

"There's a storm out there," Grant said, taking the easy way out. "With the temperatures falling it could turn to ice anytime now. Kristen's not familiar with our roads. I think I have every right in the world to be worried."

"You're sure that's all it is?"

"Yes, Evan, I'm sure that's all it is," Grant said, not about to admit how far gone he was in case he'd get another lecture.

"Good, then let's get down to business on that schedule."

After only a few minutes, Grant and Evan had come up with a remarkably easy timetable. When they factored Chas and Lily into the equation, things looked even brighter. But it wasn't until Kristen ran into the office that Grant's heart began to beat normally again.

Outrageously relieved that she had returned, he didn't fuss because her face was pale and drawn. Instead he let a swell of relief surge through him.

"Don't tell us you've come in here to quit, because we just came up with a plan that will make everybody's life easier and I'd hate to have to start all over again," Evan joked, turning to face her when she entered the room.

"No," she said quietly, then licked her lips. "I'm not here to quit. I'm here because I met Arnie Garrett today."

Grant felt his good mood evaporate. Instantly. Though he'd been very proud of himself for how well he'd handled being in the same room with Arnie at lunch, two mentions of Arnie Garrett in one day were too much to bear.

"What did he want?" Grant asked with deadly calm.

Kristen sighed, then licked her lips again. "He wants me to lie. He wants me to tell a court that you're not good custodians so he will get the kids."

Grant and his brother cursed in unison.

She took another shaky step into the room. "I'm not going to do it."

"Of course, you're not," Evan said kindly.

But Grant rose and walked over to her. He saw the shadows in her beautiful green eyes and a sort of pleading. His first instinct was to gather her into his arms and comfort her, but he ignored it. If he went too far, Evan would see his feelings and he needed to discuss marriage with Kristen alone before he announced it to the family.

"Thank you," he said sincerely, looking directly into her eyes, trying to show her how much he appreciated what she'd done, but also trying to communicate that he had deep, strong feelings for her and no matter what problem she ever had he would shelter and protect her. "Now, go take a long, hot bath, and get a good night's sleep, we'll talk in the morning."

She turned those sad green eyes on him again and for Grant it was like a vise grip around the chest. Hard to ignore. Painful. But though he knew she wanted comforting now, he knew that had to wait. He drew a breath and softened his voice. "Kristen, Evan and I have lots of things we need to discuss. You may have refused Arnie, but if he came to you with the request it means he has something up his sleeve. We can't wait until the morning to deal with this, we have to deal with it now."

Feeling his urgency, Kristen glanced from Grant to Evan and back to Grant again. The look in Grant's eyes not only brooked no argument, but it was also laced with the powerful, more private feelings rumbling between them, and told her that it would be better for them to discuss her problem alone.

In a way, she agreed with him. Though she could admit who she was and ask for help in front of Evan, the other things were best kept between only the two of them. She could wait the hour or so they would need to plot their strategy.

"Okay," she said and walked out the door, through the

foyer and into the family room where Claire sat reading a magazine.

"Kids asleep?" she asked as she, too, took a seat.

"Mmm-hmm," Claire said absently. "How was your great adventure in town?"

"Oh, Claire, don't ask," Kristen said. "I just got done telling Evan and Grant that Arnie Garrett cornered me and wanted me to lie so he could get the kids away from you."

Claire gasped. "That snake."

"Funny," Kristen said with her first laugh in hours. "That's exactly what I thought of him."

"Wanna talk about it?"

Kristen shook her head. "I think I need to talk with Grant privately first."

Her head tilted to the right, Claire assessed Kristen for a few seconds, then rose. "I think you're right. So, to get our minds off everything, how about if we have some cocoa?"

"I'd rather wait. I don't want to miss Grant."

"Honey, he'll be in that room with Evan ranting and raving for God knows how long. One cup of cocoa is not going to cause you to miss him."

Knowing Claire was probably right, Kristen followed Claire into the kitchen. Since Claire had had child care duty most of the day, Kristen insisted on being the cook. But when Claire happily allowed her to make the cocoa, Kristen got another stab of guilt. She'd begun to make friends with Claire, yet she'd also kept her identity a secret from her. She took a little comfort from the short amount of time she'd actually spent with these people, until she recognized how close she'd become with all of them in such a small span.

"Your ordeal with Arnie looks to have shaken you up," Claire observed as Kristen took a seat at the table with her.

"You could say that," Kristen agreed softly.

"Maybe you should talk about it," Claire urged kindly.

Again Kristen debated revealing her secrets, but she knew that if she told Claire first it would stab Grant's pride and then he wouldn't even be remotely open to the news. In order not to hurt or insult him, and to get his cooperation and his understanding, he had to be the first person she told.

She shook her head.

And with that one slight shake of her head, Kristen seemed to convince Claire to change the subject, because she suddenly started to talk about the adorable things the triplets had done that day. From there, Kristen and Claire moved on to discussing bits and pieces of Claire's past, her association with the lumber mill and even her employment as Norm Brewster's assistant. She could have listened to Claire talk all night about the quaint little town, with the unusual cast of characters, but when Claire yawned, Kristen immediately followed suit.

"Wow," Claire said, stretching as she rose from her seat. "I think I better take Cody and get on home."

Glancing at the clock above the stove, Kristen gasped. "My gosh! It's midnight."

Claire grimaced. "Maybe I better leave Cody sleeping exactly where he is tonight."

"I think that's a good idea," Kristen said, walking to the front foyer with Claire. "What about Evan?"

Claire smiled.

"We came in separate cars, remember?"

Just the mention of having to call Claire to come and watch the kids that afternoon washed a wave of apprehension over Kristen and she stiffened.

Claire clasped her wrist in support. "Hey, don't worry. Go to bed and when you get up in the morning everything will be fine."

Kristen shook her head. "I think I'd better wait up."

"And talk to him when you're both tired?" Claire reminded archly. "If what you have to tell him is that important I think it would be better said on a good night's sleep."

Though she was reluctant, Kristen agreed and she went up to her room, deciding that if she heard Grant before she fell asleep, she'd speak with him then. But the second her head hit the pillow she fell into an exhausted slumber and she didn't awaken until the sound of a baby crying drifted to her through the monitor.

She raced into the nursery and quickly began dressing the kids for the day, but Taylor wanted to play and Annie was unusually cranky. By the time she came downstairs, Grant was gone.

Terrified now, wide-eyed Kristen stared at Mrs. Romani. "Did he say where he was going?"

The housekeeper shrugged, turning her attention to eggs she had frying on the stove. "He's got meetings at the bank and with a subcontractor, then he said something about lunch with Evan."

"At the diner?" Kristen asked, though she didn't know of any other place since Brewster was a one-restaurant town.

"I suppose."

Kristen took a seat in front of the three babies who were pounding the trays of their high chairs, waiting for breakfast. She ran a shaking hand over her forehead. "This isn't good."

"I don't know," Mrs. Romani said, carrying three bowls of cereal to Kristen. "Maybe it's fate."

"Or maybe it's just my own stupidity coming back to haunt me," Kristen disagreed. "I should have told them the minute I arrived..."

"You came in the middle of Chas's wedding," Mrs. Romani reminded her. "That wouldn't have been appropriate."

"No, I suppose not, but later I could have—"

"Could have what? Told Grant and watched him kick you out? I don't think so. As it is, Kristen, everything was perfectly timed. You're friends now—" Mrs. Romani paused long enough to catch Kristen's gaze "—more than friends. Not only will he listen rather than react, but chances are he'll be open to helping you."

Though Kristen wasn't sure what kind of help she wanted anymore, she did agree with Mrs. Romani somewhat. Because she hadn't immediately announced who she was, she had had a chance to work her way into the Brewster lives and they now liked and trusted her. Admitting who she was might temporarily dent that trust, but nothing would change the fact that they knew her real character. When push came to shove, they liked her.

As long as she could get to Grant quickly. Before any more time passed, before someone like Arnie Garrett's secretary inadvertently leaked her identity, she had to make her confession. If he found out any other way but from her, it would ruin everything.

"I just wish I could think of a way to talk to Grant this morning."

"He's busy," Mrs. Romani said as she brought a cup of coffee to the table. "Besides, Claire's taking Cody shopping today, so she's out as a potential sitter."

Kristen raised her pleading eyes to Mrs. Romani's. "What about you?"

"What about me?"

"Could you watch the kids while I went looking for him?" Kristen asked.

"Can they do laundry?"

Kristen frowned.

Mrs. Romani playfully slapped her hand. "Of course, I'll watch the kids."

"Great, thanks," Kristen said, then jumped from her seat and unexpectedly kissed Mrs. Romani's cheek. "You're the best."

Blushing, Mrs. Romani waved away her praise. "I know. I know," she said, turning her attention to the babies. "Just go get dressed and don't blow this," she added, catching Kristen's gaze.

Looking at the older woman, Kristen felt a sudden rush of understanding. For as much as Kristen needed a little compassion, a little understanding and a great deal of help, Mrs. Romani also needed the same. Without intending to do so, Mrs. Romani and Kristen had become each other's support system.

"Go. Go!" Mrs. Romani said, again shooing her out of the room.

Reminded of the urgency of her mission, Kristen turned and darted out of the room.

She couldn't find the job site. Not being familiar at all with this heavily wooded county, every road looked the same to her. The unusual trees, which were supposed to be landmarks, didn't appear any different from the hundreds of other trees she passed as she drove down the ribbon of highway that wound through the dense forest. Most of the leaves had fallen, the tree bark was blackening in anticipation of winter, and each and every tree looked exactly alike to her. So did all of the side roads, dirt paths and big rocks that were supposed to guide her way.

It was eleven-thirty before she turned and began driving back to town. Nervous and edgy from the unproductive drive, Kristen calmed herself knowing at least she could find the diner.

At 11:55 a.m., she parked her car at the end of the

crowded street. Four minutes later, she was outside the diner door. She saw Grant and Evan seated about midway down the column of booths, and didn't give herself another minute to think. She simply pushed open the door and strode to her destination.

"Grant," she said quietly.

He looked up at the same time that Evan said, "Hey, hello. What's up?"

Grant's expression, however, was filled with alarm. "Are the kids okay?" he asked.

She nodded and attempted a small smile. "They're fine. Mrs. Romani's watching them."

While Grant breathed a giant sigh of relief, Evan started laughing. "I told you Mrs. Romani was the salt of the earth. You're not the only one with instincts. Given a little time the woman's blended right in. Here," he said, patting the bench seat beside him. "Sit, Kristen."

"No, actually, I need to talk with Grant…alone."

"Alone?" he asked quietly.

She nodded.

"Well, well, well," Arnie Garrett said, walking up behind Kristen and laying his hand on her shoulder. She almost jerked away, but before she could, he added, "What a nice picture."

"What do you want, Arnie?" Grant demanded in a low, tired voice.

Kristen guessed Arnie's intention before he could fulfill it, but because he spoke so quickly, she couldn't stop him.

"I'm happy to see you, too, Grant," Arnie said with a chuckle. "And it's nice to see that you've accepted the triplets' aunt as easily as you have. After the way you ranted about Angela, I never expected you to take in her sister like this."

It took a minute for the light to dawn for Grant, as he

was putting all the connections together, Kristen said, "Grant, I can explain...."

But his eyes widened in disbelief and his jaw slackened. "Kristen Devereaux," he said, astonishment dripping from his words. "That's where I'd heard your name. Or *seen* it. You were the next of kin contacted when Angela died."

"And given your great love for Angela, I'm sure you had no trouble forgetting that," Arnie said, placing his arm around Kristen's shoulder and squeezing lightly. "Because you didn't bother yourself with Angela's affairs after she died, you missed the fact that the triplets should have been inheriting a ranch from their mother. But Mrs. Devereaux, here, didn't miss it. And she's here to make sure the triplets get what's coming to them." He paused, giving Kristen a smile. "If I can, I'm going to help her."

Grant and Evan rose. From the way they were all standing, Kristen felt as if they were aligned for battle...and she and Grant were on opposite sides.

She shrugged from beneath Arnie Garrett's hold. "It's true that I came here to try to get my family's ranch back into Morris hands where it belongs, but I never met this man before yesterday."

Grant didn't hear most of what she said. "You lied to us."

"No, I..." *What?* If she hadn't lied, what had she done?

"She omitted a fact, Grant," Evan said, stepping in to defend her. "And I'm sure she has a good explanation," he added, giving Kristen a pointed, significant look.

"I didn't know how you'd accept me...how you'd treat me. I didn't know how I was going to get the kids away from you—"

"Get the kids away from us?" Grant hissed. "Fat chance."

"You didn't let me finish," Kristen said urgently, grabbing his forearm to keep him from walking away. By now, everyone in the diner was listening to their conversation. The hushed room seemed almost surreal.

Grant yanked his arm out of her hold. ''Honey, you are so finished,'' he said, then tossed twenty dollars down on the booth. ''If you're not out of my house by the time I get home this afternoon, the police will show you just how finished you are.''

Chapter Ten

Stung, furious, Grant strode to his black truck, Evan on his heels.

"Grant! Grant, wait!"

Only because he was at the door of his vehicle did Grant stop. If he hadn't locked it, he would have been inside and on his way before Evan caught him, not because Evan was that slow, but because Grant was that *mad*.

"Kicking her out doesn't solve anything."

Grant gaped at his younger brother. "I hope you're kidding."

Evan shook his head. "I'm not kidding. And you're obviously not thinking clearly or you would have recognized what Arnie Garrett said back there. The kids were supposed to inherit a ranch and we didn't even know it."

"So, we'll make a claim for it now."

"Don't you get it, Grant?" Evan demanded angrily. "Ranches are worth millions of dollars and we *didn't know* the kids even had the right to one. Not only do we fall short as guardians since we missed something that important, but we never investigated Angela's past, we don't know what else lurks there.''

That stopped him.

"What do you mean what else lurks there?"

Evan shrugged. "That's just the point. We don't know. If you look at this logically, we are damned lucky Kristen Devereaux showed up."

Grant snorted with disgust.

"I'm serious. In another couple of months, Arnie Garrett could have taken the knowledge that the children were beneficiaries of a ranch, but we never claimed it, and used it as proof that we were incompetent as guardians."

"And you think that could have gotten him the kids?"

"How can you be so sure it wouldn't?" Evan asked, then he stuffed his hands into his jacket pockets and sighed. "Grant, those kids had a mother, Angela. And Angela had a sister, which makes her the kids' aunt. Like it or not, Kristen is family."

"I don't like it."

"Of course, you don't," Evan said, annoyed now. "You don't like anything that interrupts your well-structured plans. Well, I have news for you, Grant. Everything in life will not go your way. And that's not your house," he added. "It's *our* house...and the kids' house...and I say Kristen stays."

"Great. Fine. Wonderful," Grant said, then jumped into the cab of his truck. "You keep Ms. Devereaux at the house for as long as you want and *I'll* find somewhere else to stay."

Grant pulled the door shut, closing out the sound of Evan cursing, and plowed down the road, out of town. He didn't know where he was going and he almost didn't care. He'd heard about people getting so angry they saw red, and for the first time in his life he understood it. If he could have harnessed all his enraged energy and put it to use, he could build the mall himself, this afternoon, with his own bare hands, that's how intense his feelings were.

After about five miles of driving deeper and deeper into the thick, black forest, Grant's anger began to ebb and in its place came his true feelings. Kristen had duped him.

The thought that she might not have meant every iota of emotion behind any one of their passionate kisses hurt Grant so much he almost couldn't handle considering it. Not because he so desperately wanted her to like him or feel passion for him, but because he himself had felt things when he kissed her that he'd never felt before and he didn't want it to be wrong. He'd poured things into his kisses, passions, emotions, wants, yearnings, everything so strong and so pure, it infuriated him to realize it had all been one-sided.

And it hurt. It hurt so much, he didn't understand it. He'd never felt pain like this before.

"He's a big man, he's a gruff man, and he's downright scary when he gets mad," Mrs. Romani said, consoling Kristen as she laid across her bed and tried not to burst into tears again.

"And he's irrational," Claire added, from her position of sitting cross-legged at the foot of the bed. "When he gets mad, he says and does things he doesn't mean."

"It's not right for him to leave his own house."

"He won't," Claire assured her, patting her hand. "He just said that in anger."

Mrs. Romani gasped. "He said he would leave?"

"I think the point was," Kristen said, sitting up so she could see her two friends, "that as long as I was here, he didn't want to be."

"Oh," Mrs. Romani said, understanding.

"Well, don't worry," Claire said. "Evan called Chas, and

Chas and Lily are flying back today. You'll have two Brewsters on your side I'm sure."

"I don't want to have *anybody* on my side," Kristen protested and rose and began to pace. "I don't want sides."

Claire sighed. "Well, there are sides. You just have to face that."

"I'm going to go talk to Grant now," Kristen said, walking to the door.

"I wouldn't," Mrs. Romani said.

"Not without Evan," Claire seconded.

Kristen shook her head. "This is really between Grant and me. I don't want your family to fight. I don't want sides."

She pulled open the door and was in the hall before anybody could stop her. Since Grant was in his room packing, she didn't have to waste time looking for him. Striding purposefully, she ate up the distance between their two rooms quickly and knocked before she had a chance to think about things.

"What?" Grant barked.

Kristen cleared her throat. "It's me. Can we talk?"

"I'm not talking to you without a lawyer present."

His calm, rational response made her blink with confusion. "What?"

"You heard me. I'm not talking to you without a lawyer."

"Is that how your family does things?"

There was a pause. A long one. Finally Grant said, "No."

She waited another couple of seconds before she asked, "Can I come in, then?"

"No."

Because his answer was quiet and strained, Kristen knew her instincts had been right. He wasn't worried about any potential threat she might pose. He was angry because of

their personal relationship. That being the case, she twisted
the knob and went into his bedroom against his wishes.

Glancing up from his packing, he looked into the mirror,
saw her reflection in the dresser and said only two words.
"Get out."

"No. I think we need to have this out. I think my not
telling you didn't make you angry as much as it hurt
you...."

Because what she was saying was true, it suddenly became all the more important for Grant to refute it. "Don't
flatter yourself."

"I'm not flattering myself. I saw what was happening
between us—"

"Nothing," Grant said, interrupting her. "Nothing was
happening between us. For Pete's sake, Kristen, we knew
each other thirteen days. *Nothing* was happening between
us."

When Grant saw her chin lift, he knew he should have
taken her short fuse into consideration before contradicting
her. At the same time, remembering that she hadn't wanted
there to be anything between them, he knew exactly how to
get rid of her.

He pivoted and caught her wrist so quickly that she didn't
see the action coming. While she was off balance and un-
steady, he yanked her against him, bent his head and kissed
her.

The second their lips met, he knew this had been a mistake. He asked himself who he was trying to torment or
baffle, her or himself, then let himself tumble headfirst into
feelings he couldn't seem to control. He loved her strength.
He loved her dignity. But most of all he loved her power.
If it came down to a recognition or admission, if only to
himself, he would have to admit that it was her power that
drew him. The funny part of it was, her power didn't lie in

strength, or size or force. Her power lay in sweetness and softness…and being right.

He wasn't sure if he meant "right" as in correct, since he knew she usually was. Or if he meant "right" as in being right for him. Equal to him. Because she was both. When he wanted to be angry, or pushy, she hauled him back.

And when he kissed her as if he had every right in the world to plunder her mouth, she answered his kiss, gave as good as she got and then some, until he softened his mouth and kissed her. Really kissed her like a man expressing feelings, not a man so unsure of himself he did stupid, macho things.

He broke the kiss and pressed his forehead to hers, holding her cheeks in the palms of his hands. "I'm sorry."

"I'm sorry, too," she whispered back. "I'm really sorry. I didn't know what to do. My family is all gone now. I had nowhere to live. I didn't know where else to turn."

Reminded of the fact that she needed him, Grant experienced a quick array of emotions. She'd done it again. Or *he'd* done it again. He'd allowed himself to fall victim to his emotions without remembering that he had no way of knowing how she felt, *what* she was feeling. She had at least three good reasons for needing him. She'd admitted she was desperate.

And she'd already lied once.

The truth was she could very well feel nothing for him. Need brought her here. Need kept her here. And need drove her to his room this afternoon. The fact that she didn't resist or refuse him was nothing more than a confirmation that her choices were limited. And if she kissed him back, kissed him desperately, it only confirmed that she was desperate. Having been acquainted for a mere two weeks, neither one of them could legitimately claim strong feelings. Because he was the older, the wiser, of the two of them, he was also the one who had to start behaving like a mature adult.

"Chas and Lily are supposed to be home tomorrow," he said, pulling back and immediately walking away from her, as far away as he could get. He never felt so foolish before in his life. Or so wrong. Because the very last thing he had to admit was that his own fling with desperation might have been what started all this in the first place.

He was to blame.

"I don't think you and I should discuss this alone. I think Evan and Chas need to be present. So, I suggest we return to our daily duties until Chas gets home, then we'll meet, then we'll see how to handle things from here."

She didn't say anything for a minute, only stared at him. He tried to avoid her, but his gaze kept straying to the mirror to catch her reflection. He saw her confusion, saw her coming to terms with his unspoken decisions, and saw her lick her lips before she said, "Does this mean you're staying?"

Unable to stop himself, he turned and looked into her eyes. "I'll stay," he said, but refused to make any further explanation—not to her or his brothers. Just the thought of having to explain fired his blood with righteous indignation. But it was the thought that people might get the wrong idea that caused him to say, "Let's not tell anyone we had this talk."

She stared at him. "Why?"

"Because you and I are not a team," he said, angry again. "Yet we keep acting as if we are and it's wrong. We're not making any decisions on our own anymore. We'll wait for the family."

Kristen understood what he was saying loud and clear. As much as she didn't want to kiss him or fall in love with him or feel anything at all for him, he didn't want to be accused of having feelings for her, either. She considered that he probably didn't want to be seen as being weak by his brothers, then instinctively knew that wasn't it. The truth was they hadn't known each other long enough to have feelings for each other. Their displays of affection always tumbled over into sexual feelings, sometimes so quickly the initial affection might not have existed. And suddenly Kristen saw that maybe it didn't.

Maybe for Grant everything pulsing between them was nothing but sex. Desire. Lust.

That would explain why he wanted to keep this secret from his brothers, particularly since he wasn't just "playing fast and loose with a nanny" as Arnie Garrett had put it, but playing fast and loose with someone his brothers considered family.

With that thought, Kristen also realized that staying away from each other, forcing their relationship into neutral, was the only way she would survive living in the same house with him knowing he had no feelings for her except sexual attraction.

Common, ordinary lust.

Her chin lifted again and she swallowed. "I'll be happy to wait for your brothers," she said. She knew she had an ally in Evan and suspected she might have an ally in Chas. She didn't expect an out-and-out fight from Grant, but she did know he had no intention of giving her anything.

Which was fine because the only thing she wanted from him was love, and he seemed incapable of that emotion.

"Lily!"

Kristen heard Mrs. Romani's affectionate cry and jumped off her bed and ran to the spiral stairway. She was only about three steps down before she got a glimpse of the couple who had cut their honeymoon short because of her.

They were *gorgeous*.

Blond, blue-eyed Lily was attractive enough that she could have graced the cover of a magazine. Demure and genuine, she bent and kissed Mrs. Romani's weathered cheek even before she removed her coat to reveal a figure that would have stopped traffic. Kristen knew it had certainly stopped her. When Claire came running out to greet Lily and Chas, Kristen was struck by the fact that both of the women who had married Brewster brothers were absolutely stunning.

But the beauty of the Brewster brides was only equal to the good looks of the Brewster men. Tall and regal, dressed in black trousers and a tweed jacket, Chas Brewster was the epitome of an educated, sophisticated man with just a hint of a tiger lurking in the depths of his pale eyes. Like his brother Evan, Chas dressed up well, presented the distinguished Brewster image, and even seemed to keep his emotions in reserve.

And then there was Grant.

When Grant came striding into the room to slap Chas's back and hug Lily, Kristen fell to a seat on the step above her. In his flannel shirt and jeans, he looked as if he'd just stepped off a log truck.

"Kristen?" Mrs. Romani called up the stairway. "What are you doing up there? Get down here with the family!"

Sudden, unexpected tears sprang to her eyes. *Family.* She didn't have a family. And if this one accepted her, it would be reluctantly—because she'd also figured out that morning that she was the key to their keeping the kids from Arnie Garrett. If he did file any kind of motion about the ranch, about the Brewsters not checking into the babies' inheritance from their mother, Kristen could be their ace in the hole.

"Kristen?" Claire called up the steps, encouraging her down.

Kristen drew a long breath and composed herself. "I just didn't want to be in the way," she said pleasantly, then started down the stairs.

Grant took over as older brother. "Kristen, meet Chas and Lily, my youngest brother and his new wife."

"How do you do?" Kristen said and extended her hand to the soft, white Lily, who, close up, was even more breathtaking than from a distance.

"I'm fine, thank you," Lily replied.

"And, Chas, Lily, this is Kristen Devereaux. She is Angela's sister and the triplets' aunt."

"It's a pleasure," Chas said, and took her hand, wrapping it warmly in both of his.

Smiling at the handsome man welcoming her into his home, Kristen felt completely ill at ease. Though it was his intention to make her feel comfortable, exactly the opposite happened. Dressed in her jeans and sweater, Kristen was nothing more than a country bumpkin standing next to the Brewsters in their pleated trousers and designer dresses. But even if you took away their monetary advantages, she didn't have Claire's thick flowing hair, or Lily's cotton candy beauty. She wasn't tall. She wasn't gorgeous. She didn't *fit* into this perfect family.

She caught a quick look at Grant in his jeans and plaid flannel shirt and tried to tell herself that wasn't true. Grant was attired as practically as she was.

But Kristen knew that though that made them equal in some respects it didn't in others. He might not look *better* than she did, but he certainly looked right. Exactly the way he was supposed to look. He was rugged, and tough and demanding.

And right now he was also something akin to her enemy.

"Well, I'm sure Kristen would like to get at least the preliminaries of this discussion over with," Grant said without preamble, directing his brothers down the hall. "Ladies, if you'll excuse us."

Kristen noticed that Claire's forehead puckered in consternation at Grant's proclamation, but she also noticed that she didn't argue.

"Let's go see the kids, Lily," she said, but she said it oddly, as if she were speaking some kind of code to her new sister-in-law.

"Right behind you," Lily said and began to follow Claire up the steps.

Grant impatiently motioned for Kristen to get moving. Not in a position where she could argue, she preceded him down the hall and took the chair he offered in front of the weathered desk in the den. She noticed he took the desk chair—his father's old chair—and that his brothers didn't sit, but rather leaned against the credenza behind him, presenting a unified front.

"I'm not here to steal the children," she said immediately.

"You couldn't get them," Chas said calmly. "Not only does our father's will appoint us guardians, but state law is on our side. Now what can we do for you?"

Since it was apparent that Chas had been filled in on the relevant details and had acquainted himself with the appropriate law, Kristen skipped right to the point. "My aunt Paige inherited my family's ranch when my uncle and father were killed in a private plane crash. Because she and my uncle didn't have children and because she isn't a blood relative, she didn't know how to bequeath the property fairly, so her will stipulated that the first of the Morris children to have a baby would get the ranch."

"Interesting," Chas said, shifting on the credenza. "So because Angela was the first to have a child, she would have inherited the ranch."

Kristen swallowed. ''No, in order to inherit, she had to live on the ranch with the child—or children.''

Chas nodded. ''You wouldn't happen to have a copy of her will?'' he asked hopefully.

She shook her head. ''No, but I'm sure I can get one.''

''I'll get one,'' Chas offered. ''It will be easier and quicker for me.''

Kristen nodded. ''Anything else?''

''No,'' Chas said. ''Before we can discuss the ranch any further I need to see the will.''

''Okay,'' Kristen said. Unsure of what else to do, she rose to leave.

''Now, the three of us need to talk about getting a new nanny,'' Grant said, and Kristen stopped on her way to the office door.

''I'm the kids' nanny.''

''You're the kids' aunt,'' Grant argued. ''You have a right to be here without having to be employed. Which means the kids need someone to care for them.''

''I care for them!''

Grant gave her a long, cool look then turned to his brothers. ''Evan, any luck with that ad?''

Evan frowned. ''Yes, but I think if Kristen's happy to care for the kids, we should let her.''

''I disagree,'' Grant said simply. ''Chas?''

Chas stared at him. ''Why would you disagree?''

''Because I need the security of knowing the kids have a real nanny,'' Grant said.

''The kids do have a real nanny,'' Chas argued.

''I agree,'' Evan seconded.

''And I abstain from voting,'' Grant said, rising from his seat. Kristen watched in horror as he strode to the door. ''You guys talk this over with Kristen and make the decision without me. I'll go along with whatever you decide. I just don't want to be a part of it."

He walked out of the room, closing the door behind him and Kristen cast a pleading look to the two remaining brothers. "I don't know what to say."

"You obviously don't know Grant very well, then," Evan said, motioning for Kristen to take her seat again. "If he can't completely control a situation he doesn't want any part of it."

"Oh," Kristen said, sitting again.

"Don't let it bother you," Chas said kindly. "It's nothing personal."

Oh, but it was. Kristen thought.

Chapter Eleven

Unlike Thanksgiving, which had been subdued because of discovering Kristen's identity, the scene in the dining room for Christmas dinner at the Brewster residence was complete pandemonium. Grant watched as his family tried to get organized and failed miserably.

To the right of the chair of each of the brothers was a high chair, which contained a screeching, hungry baby. Mrs. Romani wasn't quite sure where to sit, since she was flustered about having been asked to sit at all, and even Kristen didn't know what to do. When all was said and done, and Claire and Lily got through shifting and rearranging everyone, Grant was at the head of the table and Kristen was seated on his right.

He didn't have a problem with that, but one glance in her direction and he knew she'd rather be anywhere else. Maybe Siberia.

In the four weeks that followed his last real discussion with Kristen in his bedroom, Grant felt like he was going stark raving mad. Though he'd magnanimously gotten over being angry with Kristen for deceiving them, she hardly accepted his apology. She wouldn't speak with him unless it was about the kids. She wouldn't eat with him, unless there was a third party in attendance at the dinner. And she absolutely, positively, definitely wouldn't touch him. If their hands accidentally brushed while reaching for a comb, spoon, or washcloth, she would jump and run as if touching him somehow contaminated her.

Still, in spite of the unflattering way she treated him, he loved her and couldn't stand the fact that she was planning to return to Texas. He didn't want to go through even one day without seeing her. Contemplating the rest of his life without her was nothing but pure unadulterated torture. And not just because he would miss her, but because of the hundreds of things *they* would miss because they wouldn't be together. Private conversations. Watching the triplets learn to walk and talk. Winter in the mountains. Summer at the beach. Arguments over stupid things. Making up with apologies and kisses… And sex. He couldn't believe he'd never get to make love to her. And he couldn't imagine he'd ever want to make love with anybody else.

He didn't blame her for being angry with him, for not wanting to talk with him or even for jumping and running when he was in the room. They'd made a mess of their lives by getting involved prematurely. He recognized that this time of absolute abstinence had been necessary because it had cleared his mind to see that he hadn't imagined all the wonderful emotions she inspired in him. Everything he felt was real. Joyfully real. The problem was, now that the craziness was gone, now that solid, genuine feelings had had a chance to develop, now that he was ready to tell her he loved her for Pete's sake, it seemed she would rather be shot than have anything to do with him.

"Okay, let's say grace, already," Chas demanded. "I'm starving."

Everyone bowed his or her head, but Lily stopped the show before anyone could utter a word. "In my family, we always held hands for grace."

"Oh," Grant muttered, and watched Kristen as she glanced at his hand, then back at Lily. Being a gentleman he couldn't put her through the torment of touching him, so he said, "Well, our family's not that mushy."

"Please," Lily said, her gentile voice sugar sweet with pleading.

Grant said, "Hmm."

But Chas sighed. "Oh, come on, let's just hold hands before I die."

Suddenly preoccupied with grabbing the appropriate hands, no one noticed that Kristen and Grant were struggling with the simple task. First both put palm up. Then, simultaneously, they turned their hands over, palm down. Finally Grant sighed, caught her fingers in his and bowed his head.

Evan said the prayer of thanks, but Kristen hardly paid attention. Grant's hands were calloused, of course, because he worked. He'd had a very busy week and she'd spent an equally busy week avoiding him—just like she had every day of every week for the past four. Now they were holding hands, and feelings she'd been trying so hard to pretend didn't exist were bubbling up inside her. She was a part of this family. She'd found her babies. And she'd fallen in love. No matter how hard she'd tried to avoid or ignore it over the past six weeks it was always right there in front of her... *He* was always right there in front of her.

And that was the problem. She couldn't get her perspective because he was always around, always tempting her. Some days she just wished she could fall into his arms and beg him to love her, but she was done begging. She was done grieving Bradley. She was done grieving Angela. She would never forget either one of them, or stop loving them, but she also saw it was time to get on with the rest of her life, or she'd be vulnerable forever. She'd reasoned that being vulnerable over losing Bradley and Angela had caused her to fall in love with Grant too quickly and now she was around him twenty-four hours a day and couldn't find a way to stop loving him. She needed to get back to Texas, back to the ranch, back to her good memories and away from this man who didn't love her.

The prayer ended and Kristen had to struggle not to swipe at the tears forming in the corners of her eyes. She was tired and she was homesick. And she told herself these tears had nothing to do with her unrequited love for Grant. In the end, knowing that they would travel down her cheeks and embarrass her, Kristen casually reached up and took care of the drops of moisture. She was about to congratulate herself on successfully completing that task unnoticed, until she realized Grant had seen. Embarrassed, she focused her attention on getting her dinner, but for the rest of the evening Grant watched her. Quietly, intently, like a man looking for something specific, he watched her interact with his family.

When Mrs. Romani retired to her room, Evan and Claire left with Cody, and Chas and Lily left with Annie, Kristen wanted nothing more than to sneak up to her room. But they had Taylor to care for and Kristen herself had insisted on being the nanny, so she couldn't argue about having that responsibility.

Instead she stood by the front door, saying goodbye to Grant's family and waiting for him to give her instructions.

When he turned from closing the door on his brothers, he sighed. "You and I need to talk," he said, then shifted Taylor on his forearm.

"I know," Kristen said, fighting the urge to wring her hands. Part of her desperately wished he wanted to talk about them, about their relationship, but she knew that for him there really was no relationship. So there was nothing to talk about.

"We need to decide who will put Taylor to bed tonight," she said, as Taylor rubbed her eyes.

"No. I'm going to ask Mrs. Romani to do the honors. Why don't you wait for me in the family room?"

She would have felt much better if he'd asked her to wait in the den because the den had good lighting and a specific seating arrangement for a boss and an employee. The fact that he'd asked her to sit with him in the family room might have been a sign of acceptance, but it was also much too personal, too intimate of a room. But as he walked away to take Taylor to Mrs. Romani, Kristen nonetheless did as he requested. Within two minutes he joined her, bottle of wine in hand.

"I don't think that's a good idea," Kirsten said, ready to jump out of her skin with nerves, realizing wine made her sleepy and mellow. And soft. She couldn't be soft around this guy.

"Well, I do," Grant disagreed, handing her the glass he had just poured. He couldn't take it anymore. He knew she loved him. He could see it in her eyes, yet she avoided him as if he had the plague. And he wasn't going to tolerate it anymore.

Six weeks had taken them from being strangers and turned them into people who were very well acquainted. He ached to love, honor and cherish her for the rest of his life. And he was just plain tired of fighting it. He shouldn't have yelled at her when she confessed who she was, he should have listened to her, but he was man enough to admit he was wrong. And he was also desperate enough that he'd promise her the moon, if she'd have him back again.

But since she was the one who had been keeping them at arm's length, he also wasn't going to push. Because of the mistakes he had made in the beginning, this had to be her decision. She had to make it for herself, without prodding, because his making assumptions had taken them down all the wrong roads. He could recall at least twice that his misinterpretations kept her from confessing who she was. She'd set up opportunities and he'd ruined them by following his lust, instead of listening to what she was saying.

Tonight he vowed to listen!

He knew that it was nerves that had her bringing the cool drink to her lips. She sipped, savored the fruity liquid on her tongue, then sipped again.

Grant swallowed hard. If he didn't stop watching her, letting his mind drift to places it had no business being without her permission, he'd never get through this.

"I'm really sorry about how everything ended up between us," he said, as he took a seat on the sofa and motioned for her to sit beside him. "I take full responsibility for what happened, but I also believe it's wrong for us to avoid each other. It's time for a little honesty."

Grant didn't think he'd done such a bad job with his opening statement until she cleared her throat. "You first."

"Okay," he said, sighing. In his dreams, this would have been the point wherein she'd tell him she found him irresistible, then beg him to love her forever. Since he'd met her, however, he was constantly reminded that everything could not always go as he planned. Trying to say something that would force her to open up, he said only, "You confuse me."

She stared at him. "How could I confuse you?"

"You fit so nicely into our family that I think in the beginning I felt things for you because it was convenient."

Grant almost cursed because that wasn't anywhere near what he wanted to say, but he stopped that reaction when she peeked up at him. "I think fitting into your family might have contributed to my feelings for you, too."

Deciding that was okay, he breathed a quiet sigh of relief and set his wineglass on the coffee table. "It's good to get that part out in the open."

"Yes, it is," Kristen agreed, but she didn't say anything else. Nothing. Though Grant believed this should have been the point where she admitted that that might have been how her feelings began, but now they had changed, now they had grown, she still said nothing.

He waited.

She said nothing.

Since she obviously wasn't going to do it, Grant knew he had to make the first move. Except he wasn't exactly sure what to say or how to say it. He'd never told a woman he loved her before. And too much was at stake to say it before she was ready to hear it. He was scared and nervous and flustered to the point that what he wanted to do was kiss her. Just kiss her until she admitted she had uncontrollable feelings for him. Kiss her until she couldn't pretend indifference. Kiss her until he wouldn't have to say anything...

That thought stopped him. Not discussing their feelings was what had caused this problem in the first place. Sipping his wine, he gathered his courage, then said, "Kristen, I—"

At the same moment she said, "So, have we heard anything about the ranch yet?"

Grateful for the reprieve, Grant said, "The day Chas returned home from his honeymoon, he wrote to your aunt's attorney for a copy of the will. He figures he didn't get it yet because of the holidays. But he's sure he'll have it within the next few days and then we can set everything in motion to get your ranch.''

Kristen cleared her throat. ''It's really not my ranch,'' she reminded him softly.

''True. The ranch belongs to the kids, but now that we know our father married your sister to get that ranch for you—that it was his specific intention to do that good deed—we've decided we have to honor that. We can't simply hand it over to you free and clear, as your sister and our father might have intended. But once it's in the triplets' hands Chas says it's a simple matter for us, as the children's guardians, to make you the custodian of that piece of property for them. Chas even says we can write the documentation in such a way that you can live on the ranch forever...if that's what you want.''

He hadn't actually meant to test her, but with that last statement he had to admit he had. Never in his thirty-six years had he fallen in love. Never had he had trouble expressing his feelings, yet here he was. He was in completely foreign territory and scared witless that she was going to turn him away. If he inadvertently tested the waters, he didn't blame himself.

His tone was so casual, so cool, so indifferent, that Kristen was swamped again with the emptiness that wouldn't seem to leave her lately. She might be part of this family, they might have welcomed her with open arms, but Grant didn't feel all the wonderful things, all the runaway emotions, all the desire he'd felt for her the first two weeks she worked here. And right at this minute, she would have given anything to have him kiss her the way he had before.

But she also knew he wasn't going to. Given that he'd wanted to toss her out for deceiving him, just having a normal conversation with him was a big concession. He couldn't kiss her as if nothing had happened because a lot had happened. He might be able to forgive her. He might be able to accept her into his family. But his obvious caution this evening proved he had limits. In fact, if she looked at his offer closely, what he was doing was sending her back to Texas.

In a sense he was doing what he wanted to do all along—kicking her out...except he was doing it nicely.

Knowing going back to the ranch was what she needed, and struggling to maintain her dignity as well as acknowledge his generosity, she swallowed hard. ''Thank you,'' she whispered.

Frustrated because he'd run out of ways to try to get her to talk and was losing the battle, Grant sighed and said, ''I'm glad we could help you.''

But when she didn't respond to that, he knew the discussion was over. He couldn't believe they could go from almost being lovers to being absolutely nothing at all, but there hadn't been one iota of emotion in her voice. And now there was nothing at all for him to see in her eyes.

''Well, it's been a long day and I'm tired,'' she said, setting her empty wineglass on the coffee table.

She rose and began walking to the family room door, and Grant sat frozen with disbelief. She was going to leave him. Just like that. She was going to walk out of the room and leave him and there wasn't a damned thing he could do about it because this ball was in her court.

But halfway to the door, she changed her mind and faced him again. ''Thank you very much for everything you've done,'' she said quietly, her voice so faint and drawn he could barely hear her. ''The ranch means everything to me. Not only was I raised there, but my husband worked there. That's how I met him. It's where we courted. Once we were married, we lived there.''

Feeling a sharp stab of pain that could only be described as jealousy, Grant nodded.

"I need to go back."

Grant nodded again, and she fled the room. When he was certain she was halfway up the stairs, he punched a couch pillow and cursed. She hadn't pulled away because she was hurt or angry with him. Nor was it because she was struggling with her own feelings for him. She kept him at arm's length, because she still loved her husband.

His competition was good memories. Memories of a man she obviously adored for the past seven years. Probably memories made perfect with the passage of time.

Grant had known Kirsten six weeks now.

Actually five weeks, five days and fourteen hours... Not that he was counting.

Chapter Twelve

"I got a copy of your aunt's will," Chas said to Kristen who sat across the desk from him. Evan and Claire were seated on the sofa along the back wall. Lily leaned against the credenza behind her husband and Grant sat on the chair beside Kristen. The entire family had been gathered to hear this news, so Kristen knew it was significant.

"I've read it through and researched the appropriate law. I've even called your aunt Paige's attorney."

"And?" Grant prodded impatiently.

"And Angela fulfilled the conditions of the will simply by having the children. The part about needing to live on the ranch was more or less somebody's interpretation of a line she'd put in indicating that she'd like to see the property stay in Morris hands and she'd like to see the eventual owner live there."

"So, there's no stipulation that requires Kristen to take the kids to Texas?" Grant asked gruffly.

Chas shook his head. "Nope. The wheels are in motion for the property to be put in our names as guardians for the kids,'' he said and reached for a document to his right. ''And I've written an agreement that makes Kristen the custodian of the property for us.''

Kristen fell back on her seat. ''That's it?''

Chas nodded. ''Once Grant, Evan and I sign this, the property's yours. You can go home.''

''This is her home,'' Mrs. Romani said from the back of the room.

''Right,'' Claire said.

''Right,'' Lily seconded.

''I agree,'' Evan said.

All eyes seemed to turn to Grant. He shifted uncomfortably on his chair. ''And I think Kristen has the right to decide where she wants to live without pressure from us.''

Kristen caught his gaze. She waited to see one flicker of emotion that might make her think she'd misinterpreted their discussion on Christmas night, but his eyes were dull and lifeless, as empty as the pine tree they'd removed from the family room when the holidays were over. She hadn't misunderstood anything. He wanted her gone.

''I think it's time for me to go home,'' she said, quickly looking away.

''But you—''

''But we're—''

''The kids—''

Grant held up a hand to stop the flow of comments. ''This is Kristen's decision. Not ours. Besides, Texas is her home. That ranch is her home. Frankly,'' he said, rising from his seat, ''I think we all ought to leave her alone and let her do what she wants to do.''

With that speech, Kristen also rose. ''Then, I'm going home.''

Over the next few days everybody tried to talk her into staying except Grant. His very lack of comment became all the more obvious that he wanted her to go. But the clincher came when he surprised her with a plane ticket.

He couldn't have hurt her more if he'd come right out and told her he hated her.

So, she refused his offer to take her to the airport, accepting a ride from Lily who also brought Claire and Mrs. Romani. At the airport the four women sobbed for a good five minutes before the pilot of the small commuter insisted she board or they'd miss their connecting flights, and then it was over.

Suddenly she was seated by the window of a small, very noisy plane, waving goodbye to people she might never see again.

Because she wasn't coming back. Not again. Not ever. She would coerce Claire, Lily, Mrs. Romani or even one of the other Brewsters to bring the triplets to Texas for their visits, but as far as she was concerned, it would simply be too painful to ever see Grant Brewster again.

So she wouldn't.

She refused.

She absolutely refused.

She'd already had enough pain to last a normal person a lifetime.

"Grant, Lily just told Claire who told me that *you* bought Kristen's airplane ticket."

Grant looked up from the lease agreement he was reviewing and studied his younger brother. "So?" he asked Evan carefully, not really wishing to get into this right now. The love of his life—the only real love he'd ever had in his life—had chosen to leave him. And now he was expected to act as if he didn't care.

"So, how the hell could you do something so cruel? Did

you ever stop to think she might have thought you were kicking her out?''

"And did any of you ever stop to think that she said she wanted to leave, but she didn't have the money for plane fare?''

Confounded, Evan dropped to the chair in front of Grant's desk. "No," he said, then combed his fingers through his hair. "None of us thought of that.''

Grant leaned back in his chair. "Well, *I* did.''

Though Grant expected Evan to leave, he didn't. Before Grant could ask him to go so he could get some work done, Chas came barreling into the room.

"How could you?'' he demanded angrily.

Not needing any further explanation, Grant sighed. "She couldn't afford the ticket on her own," he said stiffly. "I hadn't intended to insult her, but to be nice to her. I'm sure that's how she took it.''

"Claire said she cried until the pilot insisted she board the plane.''

Grant did not need to hear that. "She's going to miss you guys," he said, then turned his attention to his work again.

"She's going to miss *you*," Chas said, then stormed over to the desk so he could lean over and get right in Grant's face. "And you know it," he added angrily.

Recognizing this was his moment of truth, Grant tossed his pencil onto the desk. "You guys don't know squat," he said, shoving his chair away from the desk. He wanted to bounce out of his seat, wanted to pace. Instead he leaned back and crossed his arms on his chest as if his brothers were nothing but an annoyance.

"She told me that the ranch held memories of her husband. It's where she met him. It's where she married him. It's where he died. It's where she wants to be.''

''Baloney,'' Evan said with the kind of deadly quiet Grant recognized as being very serious. ''She went back to get away from you. She went back because she thought you were pushing her out.''

''Oh, and you're the expert,'' he shot back, glaring at his brother.

''I might not be the expert but at least I didn't buy her plane ticket.''

''I did it as a kindness,'' Grant insisted, though inside his heart hurt. He kept waiting for her to refuse him. He kept waiting for her to say, ''No, I don't want this. I want to stay.'' She never did.

''You did it because you're afraid.''

''I am not afraid!'' Grant shouted, then did bounce from his seat. ''*She* was afraid.''

''*She* was head over heels in love with you but you kept kicking her out.''

Grant raked both hands through his hair. ''You guys don't know what you're talking about. She *told me* all that stuff about her husband. She told me. If I would have kept her here it would have been wrong. She still loves him.''

For a good thirty seconds, Grant watched Evan stare at him as if he were crazy. Finally he said, ''Is that what's bugging you? That she still loves her first husband?''

''It wouldn't bother you?'' Grant demanded.

Evan shrugged, but Chas answered honestly. ''Yes and no,'' he said, quietly. ''But the point is, Grant, he's gone and he's not ever coming back.''

''But she still remembers him. Still pines for him.''

Evan looked at him. ''You think so?''

''Why else would she have said that?'' Grant demanded angrily.

''To protect herself from you,'' Chas replied as if it were a simple, foregone conclusion.

"Or maybe all this smoke and mirrors is just to protect you from her," Evan speculated leaning back on his chair. "You've never been in love before, so it probably surprised you to discover that rule number one in love is that needing another person makes you vulnerable."

"That's not true," Grant mumbled even though he knew that it was somewhat true. Or at least partially true. "I can't force my way into the life of somebody who doesn't want me."

"And you're not willing to risk asking her how she feels, either," Evan said, getting a little angry himself. "Because of your foolish pride, you were afraid to ask. Afraid to get rejected. So you made up this scenario in your head that gave you a way out." He crossed his arms on his chest. "So now you're out," he said, catching Grant's gaze. "How does it feel?"

"Miserable," Grant admitted honestly.

"Then go get her," Chas said.

"You don't understand," Grant began, but Evan stopped him.

"No, you don't understand," he said and walked to the door of the den. "This is it. If you don't go after her, then you don't love her. If you really loved her you wouldn't be able to keep yourself from going after her."

He turned to walk out of the room, but stopped himself and faced Grant again.

"Don't think you're taking your bitterness, anger or resentment out on the rest of us. I thought we all learned our lesson about being stubborn two years ago when Dad married Angela. I guess I was wrong."

Chapter Thirteen

When Kristen arrived in Texas, it was like entering another world. Though the hustle and bustle of the business end of the ranch was alive and well and functioning as if nothing had happened, the house was cold and empty. She stepped inside, smelling the cool, musty scent of barrenness and wondered if this wasn't the rest of her life. Except for visits from the triplets, she couldn't envision this big house with the echoing corridors being filled with any kind of laughter or love. Not because she didn't want love, but because she'd had a second chance at love, but it slipped through her fingers.

And she wasn't trying again. Not ever. Even the trying hurt too much.

She spent the first week reinstalling utilities, consulting with staff, checking in with Aunt Paige's lawyer and eventually calling Chas. She wasn't sure whose idea it was, but somehow or another she was now the president of this multimillion-dollar operation. The ranch had been turned into a corporation with layers and layers of employees *she* was supposed to supervise. Though she was eternally grateful for something to do, the job seemed momentous, overwhelming.

"Technically you are the manager," Chas told her over the phone. "As manager you can do anything with this company that you want. Even hire or fire anyone as you see fit. This is your property, Kristen. As president you also earn a salary. So there's a lot at stake here for you," he said with a laugh. "That's why we gave you both the position and the authority. But, in our opinion, there isn't anything that needs to be done with the way the ranch business is handled. The employees who are in place must be doing well because everything's running smoothly and the business is making money. Both Grant and I went over the books and records to confirm that."

The mention of Grant's name stopped her heart, but she tried to be casual. "Well, that's good. It sounds like I'll have at least a couple of months to get my feet wet before I need to make any important decisions."

"You have plenty of time," Chas assured her. "And even if you do have a problem, you have lots of resources at your disposal. Don't forget, Evan's a certified public accountant. I'm a lawyer. And Grant's just plain smart. He has business savvy the rest of us dream of having. Anything, absolutely any problem you have, Grant can solve."

With the second, more obvious reference to Grant, Kristen grew weak with longing. She leaned back on the chair behind the metal desk of the ranch office. Where the Brewster den had been stately and ornate, rich and alive with woods and expensive rugs, the office in the ranch house seemed like something of an afterthought. The walls were paneled with a light pine, the furniture was old and worn, the filing cabinets were utilitarian metal.

"If you're having trouble getting adjusted, maybe you

should call him for advice. He could help you set up things. He could tell you what to say when you meet with the employees and announce that you're everyone's new boss."

Kristen licked her dry lips.

"He's really good with things like this, Kristen."

Kristen cleared her throat. "Yeah, I know."

"So, give him a call," Chas said brightly, but Kristen found herself wishing that he wasn't giving this advice as a business consultant, but as a brother. She fervently wished Grant was as miserable as she was.

But she also knew that if he was, he would do something about it.

"I don't think so. Maybe I'll talk with Evan first."

Chas sighed. "Come on, Kristen, have a heart. I don't know what happened between the two of you, but you're both miserable. You're sad and alone and he's sad and surrounded by people who pester him day and night. Except now he doesn't have anybody to share the burden with."

"Is that what I was?" Kristen asked softly. "Someone he shared his burdens with?"

"Hell, I don't know. I'm not even sure the two of you know. I only know that both of you are equally miserable." He sighed. "Just call him."

It took two days of walking around the ranch, acclimating herself to her new station in life and wrestling with herself, but in the end Kristen decided to take Chas's advice. Not because she needed Grant's help. Surprisingly, she knew much more about running a ranch than she'd imagined, mostly because she'd been born and raised here. Dinner conversations were miniclasses. And problems were typically solved using good old-fashioned common sense. She knew there would be times when she would need the help of Evan, Chas and even Grant, but in general she would do more than okay in her new job.

So when she picked up the phone and dialed Grant's number, it was more because she was hoping, praying, he needed her emotional support than because she needed his business acumen.

"Hi," she said, when he finally came to the phone.

"Hi," he said, sounding surprised and confused and maybe even pleased.

She drew a long breath for courage and said the line she'd rehearsed all morning. "Chas explained my position here at the ranch and also told me that if I had a problem I was to call him, Evan or you."

He didn't give her a chance to go any further. "You have a problem?" he asked, almost panic-stricken.

"Well, no," she said, then wished she'd started the whole conversation differently. Now he thought she was a ninny who couldn't handle the job they'd given her.

"That's good," he said quickly—so quickly Kristen's forehead furrowed with confusion. Then she remembered the other thing Chas said about Grant being overburdened with other people's problems. In a sense, she'd been nothing but one of those problems. And here she was again. Calling him. Leaning on him.

She deliberately packed all the strength and confidence she could into her voice. "I just called to more or less update you on how everything's going down here and—" she paused, gathered her courage again "—to tell you that you don't have to worry about me anymore."

There was silence on the other end of the line. Cold, dead silence. Finally Grant said, "Good. Great. Wonderful. I wanted to hear that you're doing well. This could be the start of a whole new life for you. That ranch is a big responsibility, but it's also an awesome opportunity. I'm glad we could help you."

Something about his words was so final that it hit Kristen

right in the heart. She'd been dismissed by him more curtly and more obviously, but she'd also been around him long enough to know that the kinder, gentler words were still a dismissal.

"Thank you," she said, then swallowed hard. Tears were already gathering in her eyes. Her throat was closing. He didn't need her. He didn't even want her. Anything that might have been between them was gone as far as he was concerned.

"Well, I guess I've gotta go," she said shakily. "Thanks again for your help."

She didn't wait for him to say goodbye. She couldn't bear it. Instead she quickly hung up the phone, then laid her head on her folded arms and let herself cry.

She now had absolutely everything she wanted. The ranch. Money. Position. Power. Even family, because of the triplets. But the one thing she hadn't set out to get was the one thing she finally realized she needed the most.

Grant's love.

But it was gone…he was gone. He'd taken himself away from her because he couldn't trust her anymore.

Grant squeezed his eyes shut as he hung up the phone and wondered why he'd ever thought that woman needed him. He couldn't understand why he'd ever been so arrogant as to believe anything would push her back to him when challenges only seemed to make her stronger.

Then he wondered what the hell he was going to do without her for the rest of his life.

"You know, Grant," Mrs. Romani said from the doorway of the den. "In some ways I can understand what you're feeling about Kristen."

Good for you, Grant thought, too tired, too hurt, too beaten to even answer.

"But part of me thinks you're crazy."

At that Grant burst out laughing. He should have known better than to think anyone was on his side.

"If I'm the one who is supposedly in control of this mess," Grant said, taking Taylor from Mrs. Romani's arms when she brought the baby to him. "Why the hell does it hurt so much?"

"I don't know," Mrs. Romani said, then sat on the seat across from his desk. "Why don't you tell me?"

Playing with Taylor, Grant avoided her gaze. "It might be because Chas's description of the man she hired to do the audit of the books since her aunt Paige's death made him sound like Adonis in boots and a Stetson."

Mrs. Romani only stared at him. "You're jealous."

"No kidding," Grant retorted. "Keep up, here, Mrs. Romani. If anybody should have guessed that it should have been you."

"Well, I knew you liked her. I just figured that if you liked her so much you'd get heartsick and jealous over people you haven't even met that you wouldn't sit around here brooding, you'd do something about it."

"Like what?" Grant countered.

"Like go down there and tell her how you feel."

Grant gaped at her. "She doesn't want me. She all but told me that she doesn't need me. I'm sure as hell not going down there to make a fool of myself."

For a good thirty seconds Mrs. Romani only stared at him. Finally she said, "Oh, I get it now."

"Wonderful," Grant said. "Then share it with the class, because the rest of us don't have a clue."

"You're mad because you don't have the control."

"That's preposterous."

"Is it?" Mrs. Romani asked archly. "When I first started here, Grant, what was our problem?"

He gave her his patented don't-confuse-the-issue stare. "You wanted to run the show."

"Precisely," she agreed easily. "But *you* liked to run the show."

Conceding that with a nod, he gave her permission to continue, though he thought she was talking nonsense.

"At issue here, Grant, is your pride. If you admit to Kristen that you love her before she tells you, you make yourself vulnerable. But more than that, I think you think if you say it first she controls you."

Though his brothers had said something similar, Grant disagreed. "There's more here," he insisted. "She has a first husband whom she still loves. I'm second. I'll always be second."

"That's very convenient, but I don't buy it. First of all, if she didn't hold some special place in her heart for her late husband she wouldn't be the woman you love. So there's a part of you that respects that."

Though he'd never looked at it that way before, he had to admit that was true. "All right," he agreed tersely.

"Second of all, Grant, her first husband is dead. He's not competition. He's memories and she deserves to keep them."

When she said it like that, Grant got an uncomfortable feeling of immaturity and irrationality.

"So even though you can more or less lean on those for convenient excuses the real truth is this is a control issue for you. You are afraid to be vulnerable."

"Look at me, I'm ten years older than she is. I have responsibilities that would make any woman cringe with fear that she'd never see me and when she did I'd be grouchy and moody. I leaned on her in a way I never leaned on anybody before...." Grant caught Mrs. Romani's gaze. "And where did it get me? She ran. She left me."

"You bought her a plane ticket, Grant," Mrs. Romani reminded him.

"Only so she could refuse it," Grant quietly admitted. "But she didn't refuse it. She took it and left. To me that's proof she doesn't want me."

"To her it was proof you wanted her to go."

Grant looked up sharply. "I wanted her to stay."

"Did you tell her?"

He shook his head.

"Then go tell her now." Mrs. Romani rose. "Just get on a plane, take yourself to Texas and tell that woman you love her. You might be very surprised at what she tells you in return."

"And what the heck are we supposed to do with the kids while I'm in Texas?"

She stared at him. "Grant, don't ask me. It's your life. If you're willing to throw it away because you can't find a baby-sitter I refuse to be a party to it."

The next morning when Kristen stepped out of the corral after her walk, she saw a strange truck parked in front of the house. Though it took a while to make the trip to the porch, she never saw anyone get out of or go back to the truck, so she knew whoever it was had been there a while and she also knew the person must be waiting to see her or they would have gone by now.

Hurrying her steps, she made it to the porch quickly, but came to an abrupt halt when she saw luggage piled by the door. Her first thought was that the California Morrises hadn't been given the word yet that the triplets' claim to the ranch was valid, but when she saw three baby swings, her heart stopped.

She followed a trail of walkers, diaper bags and high

chairs that wove a path through the foyer to the kitchen where all three babies were sitting in carriers on her floor.

And right beside the kids were a man's feet.

Grant's feet.

Slowly, cautiously, she looked up at him.

"Hi."

She could only stare at him. "Hi," she echoed, so confused she couldn't talk. A million questions sprang to mind, but the slapping and gooing of babies overrode everything else. "How did you manage to travel with three babies?"

"With the help of my housekeeper."

At the mention of her name, Mrs. Romani stepped out of the first floor powder room. "Hi!" she said, then grabbed Kristen and gave her a big hug. "So," she said, looking around. "This is Texas."

"A piece of it," Kristen confirmed happily.

"A great big piece of it," Grant reminded her.

"Right," Kristen said, finally understanding what was going on. "You're here to check up on me because I called you."

"You could say that," Mrs. Romani agreed, reaching for Cody, whom she handed to Grant. "He's definitely here to check up on you." She grabbed Taylor and easily gave her to Grant, before she picked up Annie. "Hope you don't mind, but Grant and I already assigned some nice young man to set up cribs. Since these kids are ready for a nap, I'm going upstairs to make sure everything gets done quickly. Grant's coming with me because he has to carry two kids. He'll be down in a minute. You put on coffee."

Because everybody had gotten accustomed to Mrs. Romani giving orders, everyone shifted and moved without question. But Kristen barely had the water poured into the reservoir of the coffeepot before Grant returned to the kitchen.

Fully expecting a stern lecture, she turned to him with a glare. "Chas told me that I could handle this ranch any way I wanted," she said, fuming with indignation. *How dare he travel two thousand miles to yell at her!* "Because this job is my future. *My* future."

"Your future can be anything you want it to be."

Her eyes narrowed. "Now what the hell are you talking about?"

From the tone of his voice, she could almost believe he'd changed his mind about her running the ranch. "You're not taking this ranch away from me."

"I don't want to take this ranch away from you, but really, you're needed at home."

She stared at him. "I am home."

He shook his head. "No, your home's in Pennsylvania now...with me."

That stopped her heart. It stopped her brain. Every rational thought she had slid out of her head like melted Jell-O on a warm day.

"Come home, Kristen, we miss you."

"We?" she asked, though she wasn't entirely sure how she managed to find her voice.

"I," he corrected quietly, reluctantly. But he caught her gaze and with a firmer voice said, "*I* miss you. *I* need you. *I* didn't want you to leave."

"Why?"

Grant almost cursed her in his head because she wouldn't give an inch. But he tried to think of things from her perspective as Mrs. Romani had instructed him to do. She was alone. She had nothing. No one. For someone who was proud and unpretentious—someone who was very much like him—both of those would be hard. She wouldn't take anything for granted. She certainly wouldn't beg.

He couldn't stand the thought of her begging. He couldn't

stand the thought of her alone. He couldn't stand the fact that he was the author of most of her misery.

"I love you," he said easily, almost automatically, because easing her pain suddenly became more important than protecting himself. He realized he'd face any enemy for her, fight any demon or dragon to protect her. And with those realizations came blessed relief, almost joy.

He grinned. "I love you," he said again, if only because it was so easy, so wonderful.

"I love you, too," she whispered and inside Grant felt everything turn to rubber.

"Then come here," he said and held out his arms, but he didn't wait for her to walk to him. He took two steps. She took two steps and they were in each other's arms. He never felt so gloriously happy, so gloriously alive, so gloriously everything.

He didn't think about kissing her, he just did. And she didn't think about responding, for them it seemed all that came naturally.

When he pulled away, though, he was frowning. "So where's the guy you hired to audit the ranch books?" he said, and Kristen could hear his jealousy dripping from every word.

"George?" she asked, then began to giggle. "He's seventy-two, walks with a cane and only wears a Stetson because he can't tolerate the sun anymore."

Grant's eyes narrowed. "You know, I'm going to have to kill Chas and Evan for this."

Kristen peeked up at him from beneath her lashes. "Personally I think we should thank them."

Grant looked down at her. He was holding everything he'd ever wanted, everything he'd ever need in his arms.

They'd get married. They'd raise Taylor. They'd have kids
of their own. They'd argue. They'd tussle. They'd make
love. Things would never be dull for them.

He grinned. "Yeah. Actually I think we should."

Epilogue

Kristen wanted to get married in the summer, Grant felt Valentine's Day was a much better choice. They compromised and were married the first day of spring in the gardens behind the house. Though only the lilacs were blooming, their scent brought an air of romance to the place. Flooded in sunlight and surrounded by friends, Grant and Kristen made the commitment both knew would easily last a lifetime. For better, worse, richer, poorer, neither one of them had any doubt that they'd pull it off.

Over a year old, the triplets were now walking, but Mrs. Romani didn't have any trouble keeping them in line. Abby Conway had been enlisted as her assistant for the day, but even Abby didn't feel there was any need for her to stay by General Romani's side. She mentioned it to Grant, who took one look at the situation and gave her a reprieve, but Kristen couldn't help but notice that rather than mixing and mingling with the crowd, Abby found her son and spent the rest of the afternoon with him.

"What's the deal with Abby?" she asked Claire and Lily

when the three of them retired to her room to help her change into traveling clothes for her honeymoon with Grant in the Bahamas.

"What do you mean, what's the deal?" Claire asked, unzipping Kristen's antique lace gown.

"I've never seen her with anybody but you, Claire, or her son, Tyler."

Claire and Lily exchanged a look, and Claire said, "That's because she still loves Tyler's father."

"Oh," Kristen said, embarrassed. "I shouldn't pry."

"Well, actually, *you* should pry," Lily interjected. "Because Tyler's father is Grant's partner."

"What?" Kristen asked incredulously.

"And if anybody's got a shot at getting Hunter home, it's Grant. But don't fuss and don't worry," Claire said, hanging Kristen's gown in her closet and then helping her slide into the jacket of her pink suit. "We'll fill you in when you get back. You just enjoy your honeymoon."

"As if she has a choice," Lily said with a giggle.

"I know," Claire agreed, then sighed. "Bahamas. Sun. Fun. I wish I could go with you."

"I'm glad you can't," Kristen said, laughing, and started for the door. "I don't think Grant and I have had two minutes of peace and quiet since I returned from Texas."

"We like you," Lily said simply, following Kristen out the door.

"Yeah, we like you," Claire seconded, two steps behind Lily.

When Kristen arrived at the top of the stairs, the wedding guests were waiting for her to throw her bouquet. She turned her back on the crowd and gave the floral arrangement a Texas-size toss and pivoted just in time to see the flowers land in Abby's arms.

Both Lily and Claire screamed with delight and went running down the steps, and Kristen took advantage of the opportunity to slip back to the den, where Grant awaited her.

She closed the door quickly and leaned against it with a sigh. "Alone."

"Not for long," Grant said and scooped her off her feet. "We have to be at the airport in twenty minutes. The way I have this figured, we'll only get through the crowd if we make a surprise run for it. Since you've only got those little Texan feet and I've got these long Pennsylvanian legs, I'm our best bet for catching our flight."

Just because she'd been waiting all day to be alone with him, Kristen kissed him. What started out to be a quick peck on the lips, grew and lingered and turned into full-scale sexual assault. When she finally pulled away both of them were breathing heavily.

"How long do we have before we miss our flight?"

"Ten minutes," Grant replied, staring at her with smoky, hazy brown eyes. "If I make a couple of calls, I could probably get them to hold the commuter for half an hour, maybe forty minutes."

She nodded toward the door. "Does that lock?"

He grinned. "Yeah."

"You make the call. I'll lock the door," she said and slid from his arms. "Last one on the sofa has to tell your family we decided to spend two weeks in the Bahamas instead of one."

*   *   *   *   *

Look for more books from talented author
Susan Meier in 2000 in Silhouette Romance

Look Who's Celebrating Our 20th Anniversary:

"Happy 20th birthday, Silhouette. You made the writing dream of hundreds of women a reality. You enabled us to give [women] the stories [they] wanted to read and helped us teach [them] about the power of love."

—*New York Times* bestselling author
Debbie Macomber

"I wish you continued success, Silhouette Books.... Thank you for giving me a chance to do what I love best in all the world."

—International bestselling author
Diana Palmer

"A visit to Silhouette is a guaranteed happy ending, a chance to touch magic for a little while.... It refreshes and revitalizes and makes us feel better.... I hope Silhouette goes on forever."

—Award-winning bestselling author
Marie Ferrarella

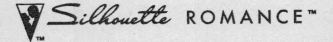

Visit us at www.romance.net

PS20SRAQ1

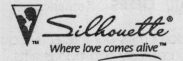